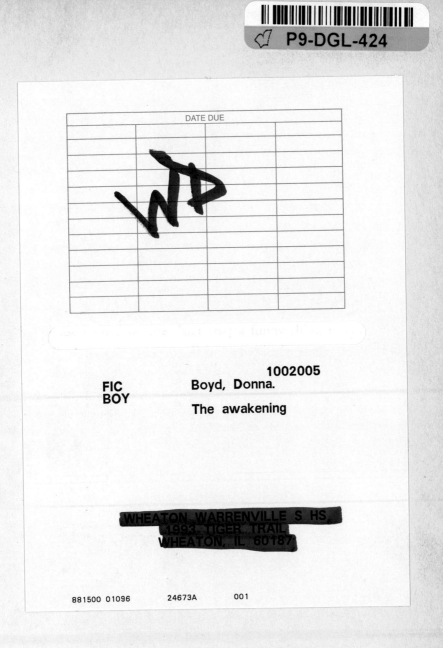

DATE DUE

1002005

FIC
BOY

Boyd, Donna.

The awakening

881500 01096   24673A   001

THE
AWAKENING

Donna Boyd

Ballantine Books • New York

A Ballantine Book
Published by The Random House Publishing Group

Copyright © 2003 by Donna Ball, Inc.

www.ballantinebooks.com

Library of Congress Control Number: 2003090237

Cover illustration by Phil Heffernan/PHX

ISBN 0-345-46235-1

Manufactured in the United States of America

First Edition: July 2003

2 4 6 8 10 9 7 5 3 1

AWAKENING

ONE

If a human being is the sum total of all her thoughts, memories, and experiences, then I was, for some indeterminate period of time, nothing. I did not exist. I hovered on the edge of consciousness like a breath waiting to be drawn in, a dream not quite formed into images, almost alive and not quite dead. It was not a particularly disagreeable state. Those who know nothing want for nothing, and it was good, for a time, simply not to care.

And then I began to awaken.

My memories of those first days are blurred and tossed together like fruit spilled from a basket; some moments, the brightest in color, stand out in particular; others are lost altogether; none are in the correct order. My eyes, so long unused to seeing, struggled to separate amorphous clouds of light into faces and objects, and did not always succeed. My ears could not quite distinguish one sound from another, and the background noise formed a rather soothing hum of almost musical cadence.

I whispered the customary words, surprised at how hollow and faraway my own voice sounded. "Where am I?"

A face floated into view, familiar, kind. But I could not say I recognized it.

"Don't you remember?"

I sensed a disappointment when I did not answer, although the voice was carefully neutral. "Try to remember. You've been awake before. You've asked the question before. Try to remember what happened."

But the gentle winds of void were beckoning to me again, and remembering seemed entirely too much trouble. I whispered, "I want to go home" just before I drifted away again.

And so it was, the same scene repeated over again, I can't say how many times. I would awake, I would question; I would sleep, I would forget. But gradually, it seemed, I stayed awake longer, I forgot less. Memories drifted through my dreamlessness like dandelion fluff on a summer breeze.

A house with a green shutter that banged in the wind. A garden and a stone frog covered in moss. The smell of baking bread. A starched doily on a cherry table. Rain on the roof. A child's voice.

Scraps of a life, bits of a woman. Particles of chaff, harmless and pretty as they danced in the sun, drifting closer and closer until I could see they weren't chaff at all but floating moths with gossamer wings; no, not moths and not floating, but buzzing insects, darting and daring, irritating me, teasing and stinging and drawing me back to a place I didn't want to be.

I opened my eyes to the hurtful light. I kept them open. And this time I asked a different question. "What's wrong with me?"

The face was back, kind and concerned. A male face, familiar. That's all I can tell you about it. "What can you remember?" he asked.

"What's wrong with me?" I repeated, more forcefully now. "You can tell me. My husband is a doctor."

Ah, that I should know that. It was a milestone, and I recognized the fact as well as he did.

"You've suffered a severe trauma," he said gently. "There was a great deal of damage, I'm afraid, to your cognitive functions, and most particularly to your memory. We've all been very worried."

A vague uneasiness crept through me, like beetles crawling on my skin. This time I couldn't make it go away by slipping back into the nothing place. "How long?"

His eyes were sad and guarded. "A long time."

Too long. I knew it in my bones. Too terrifyingly long. "Months?"

Silence pulsed like a heart, muffled and strained, whispered like a wind gathering force in the distance, fading, swelling. There were no words, no answers, but I found I did not need them. He just looked at me with those sad eyes, and certainty was like a cold, dark ribbon twining around my soul. I knew.

Too long.

"WHO ARE YOU?"

This time it was I who asked the question, as we strolled some days or weeks later in the garden of what I had come to understand was the sanitarium where I had been admitted after the accident. I continued to be baffled by the indefinite control I possessed over my body, as though limbs, muscles, and responsive nerves had also been afflicted with spotty memory loss. Sometimes I strolled, sometimes I stumbled; sometimes I glided, sometimes I could not move at all no matter how hard

I tried. I might reach for something and grasp only air. I might desperately *want* to reach for something, and be unable to move at all. The sweet-faced nurses and therapists assured me this all was normal, and that I was making a remarkable recovery. Perhaps. In truth, the challenges of learning to motivate through my environment, of envisioning an action and then performing it, seemed but minor inconveniences to me. I was far more concerned with what had been lost inside my mind.

Scraps of understanding were returning to me, though in no particular order and without a great deal of meaning. I knew, for example, that it had been an accident that was responsible for my injuries, but I did not know what kind of accident, nor how extensive those injuries were. I remembered the terror of that moment, the violence and suddenness of it, and even, to some startling extent, the pain. But I could remember no details.

I knew I was in a sanitarium, although I did not know how I knew it, and I did not know where, nor for how long. I did not know my age or my name or my station in life, nor what I looked like nor who were my friends nor who was my family. No one came to visit me. Had they all forgotten me? Or had there never been anyone at all who cared? Did I play the piano or like to dance? Who were my favorite authors? How did I like to pass the time on a lazy summer day? What kind of life had I had that I could leave it so easily and forget it entirely?

Sometimes questions like these consumed me with a feverish intensity; other times I didn't care at all. Sometimes answers would come to me, as surprising as a suddenly popped balloon, with no warning whatsoever. Most of the time there were only questions.

The attendants at this place whose name I did not know

were of precious little help. It was against policy, they said, to supply any answers about a resident's past. It was very important that everything I learned be the result of spontaneous recollection; only in this way could my recovery be considered permanent and genuine.

So I had learned to mask my questions in innocuous forms, like "Who are you?" and to hoard every scrap of information that was returned to me against that time when I might have enough pieces of the puzzle to begin to put together a shape.

He said, with a firm and reassuring smile, "I am the person who is going to help you get better. You can call me Michael."

"You're a doctor." A statement of the obvious. "I'm not comfortable calling you by your Christian name. It seems disrespectful."

"It's not, I assure you."

We were in the garden because I longed so for the scent of clean air and the touch of the sun, for the lush ripeness of growing things and fecund earth. But the experience so far had been less than satisfactory. The colors seemed muted somehow, the greens flat and the yellows brown. The flowers had no scent. The light did not warm.

I knew there were medications that could dull the senses. But I was terrified by the thought that this muffling, foggy veil that seemed to have twined itself around my brain like spiderwebs on a dewy morning was nothing that could be induced by an injection or erased with a pill. The damage might be permanent. I might never again hear the trill of a chickadee in all its subtle nuances, or smell the perfume of spring grass, or gasp with delight over the shadow a butterfly cast on a stone path in late-summer light. The possibility filled me with such dread that I could not even ask for the truth of it.

I said, "My husband was a doctor, you know."

"Yes, I know."

"He was a brilliant man."

We walked through the still and colorless garden with its soft, cool light and its pale flowers. I felt the comfort of Michael's presence beside me, but it seemed a small thing, floating alone in a great hollow universe. I said softly, "He's dead, isn't he?"

"Yes." Without hesitation, without apology. It was as though he were observing that the sky is blue, or remarking how lovely the forsythia was this year. *Yes.*

It was not so much sorrow that filled me, but a swelling sense of loss, a wave that crested and broke and was lost again in the sea of my despair. I wanted to weep, but could not find the tears. And I was shamed by the almost certain knowledge that, if I did cry, it would not be for the man whose face I could not remember, but for myself. He was dead. I think I had always known that.

I said, "It was the same accident that took my memory. There were no survivors." Odd, how I simply said that, and knew it was true. Something else I must have always known.

We walked for a long time in empty silence. I said, "I'm all alone."

"Of course you're not. Everyone here wants to help you."

"But they can't, can they?" Now I turned and looked directly into the kind face of this man I did not know, but who was the only familiar thing in a world of void. "No one can help me. I think I must have read about places like these, people like me. No one ever gets better. No one ever goes home."

"That's not true. You're going to get better."

"Then help me!" I cried. "Tell me what happened to me, tell me what I've lost, tell me how he died! Tell me where I am and where I came from and what I have to do to get my memory back! Tell me who I am!"

"I can't do that," he said gently. "Only you can do that."

I felt for a moment a powerful surge of anger, an emotion so genuine that it startled me. For just that instant, colors were bright and scents were sharp and I thought I caught the buzz of a honeybee. But in less than the space of a breath it all was gone, anger fading into helplessness like fog into mist. I said, turning away, "Then there's no hope for me. I can't even remember my name."

"Do you want to remember?" he asked.

A strange question, and a terrible one. It took me a long time to form a reply, for the answer was even more frightening than the question. I could not meet his eyes when I spoke it. "I don't know."

"What you do want, then?"

This time the answer came quickly, and with a fervency I had not expected. "Home," I said. "I want to go home."

"Why?"

I said, "Because everything is there. The answers are there."

"The answers are here," he replied tenderly. "I think you know that."

"No," I whispered, fighting back a surprising urgency I did not entirely understand. "I can't stay here. I don't belong here."

He smiled the way one smiles at a child one is trying to comfort or reassure. "Where do you belong?"

Sorrow settled through me like a weighted thing; it dragged at my feet and held down my arms and filled up my center until even the act of speaking was too much to manage. I did not know. That was the worst of it. I didn't know.

*　　*　　*

THE HUMAN BRAIN is divided into four lobes, each associated with a specific function. Injury or disease within a specific lobe, or a portion of the lobe, can disrupt the functions associated with it in either a generalized or very specific way; sometimes temporarily, sometimes permanently. A tumor in the language center, for example, might cause aphasia—the inability to speak—but leave the patient entirely capable of understanding the spoken word. A chemical imbalance in the portion of the brain that processes information might render a man incapable of distinguishing certain ordinary objects of a very specific type—those with a linear shape, for example, like walking canes or trees—but leave him perfectly functional in every other way.

The memory centers, likewise, can be divided into very specific areas of long- and short-term memory, and within those categories are even smaller, more precise sections which are associated with categories, groups, and even individual memories. Imagine a portion of the brain no larger than the head of a pin. Excise it, and there goes the memory of your sixth birthday party. Move on to another area, and erase the ability to do complex mathematics.

Amnesia is a general term that describes the loss of memory, and usually refers to the most common type: global, or autobiographical, amnesia. In this type of amnesia one may very well retain all learned skills and common associations, but lack any recognition of one's self. Name, place of birth, family, friends, job—even one's own face in the mirror—are completely unfamiliar. Although the victim of this kind of amnesia may eventually relearn the details of his life and his identity, a spontaneous and full recovery is rare.

In other forms of amnesia, the sense of self remains intact, but learned skills—the ability to read, write, or tie one's shoelaces—are destroyed. In other cases, the ability to recognize and place in context certain commonplace components of everyday life may be affected, or the ability to replicate learned behaviors. Short-term memory may be intact or even enhanced, enabling the victim to recite long lists within moments of memorizing them, but rendering him incapable of recognizing his own family from one day to the next. Or long-term memory may be unaffected, but the ability to remember an address long enough to write it down, or to recall whether one has locked the front door only seconds after having done so, is diminished.

It is a highly complex and largely unexplored topic, the human brain. And I had been studying.

Autobiographical amnesia may be caused by head injury, high fever, a chemically induced neurological imbalance, emotional or psychological trauma, hysteria. In the case of the last set of circumstances, memory may often be recovered when the trauma is overcome, as no actual brain cells have been destroyed. When the cause of the amnesia is physical damage to the brain, however, the memory loss is permanent. Brain cells are destroyed, and the memories they once held are gone. One cannot recover what does not exist.

Memories were returning to me. Slowly, faintly, and with a maddening lack of consistency, they were returning. Today I remembered a pearl button on a gray silk dress that had come loose in my hand on a busy morning. Tomorrow I might remember my address, or when I was married . . . or to whom.

Michael said, "Memory and imagination are linked, you know, in ways we don't always understand. It's often difficult to be certain how much of what we remember is real, and how much is simply the imagination filling in the details."

It infuriated me that he refused to share my triumph over the pearl button. "I remember it distinctly. I was standing in front of a window, buttoning my dress. There was a white curtain at the window, and a breeze that billowed it. Springtime. Yes. Just a little cool, but green outside. I could hear dogs barking and church bells ringing and the voice of a child in another room. I turned to answer her, and that was when the button came off in my hand." Even in the telling, details began to fill themselves in for me, and I was excited by the process.

"Describe the room in which you were standing," Michael said.

I hesitated. "It was a bedroom," I said. But was it? Or was it simply that the bedroom seemed a logical place for one to stand while dressing? "The floors are dark polished wood and the walls are white. There's a bed with a white counterpane."

"What kind of bed?"

I was impatient. "What do you mean, what kind of bed?"

"Metal or wood? Four-poster or carved headboard? Painted or plain?"

I did not know, and my frustration level rose. He looked sympathetic. "Perhaps there is a table there," he said, "with a vase of flowers. Perhaps they are yellow."

I could see them. "Daffodils."

"Or perhaps they are pink. Perhaps there is no table at all, and no vase, and the daffodils that, only a moment ago, you saw so clearly never existed. The imagination is a desperately accommodating facility, and will eagerly supply whatever details we require of it to support the reality we envision."

"Then you're saying there never was a window," I said angrily, "or a spring morning with children playing, or a broken button. That I invented it all to entertain myself."

"No," he replied gently. "I'm not saying that at all. I merely meant to demonstrate how very elastic are the borders within which we define reality. And to encourage you to ask yourself again, perhaps, how much you really want to remember."

Oh, how blithely the words rolled off his tongue, how carelessly they toppled the pillars of my universe. I could feel temper, with its flash of fire that did not burn, rise in my gorge. "You're not a doctor at all," I accused recklessly, and made as though to storm theatrically away. "You're a cruel and impotent little man who has no intention of helping me remember. I refuse to listen to any more of your twisted nonsense, and I demand that you let me go home immediately!"

It was his calm that arrested me, his unruffled certainty. "You would not be comfortable there," he said. "Everything would seem strange to you. You would have difficulty functioning. You're not ready to go home."

Hardly words of encouragement, and yet I could not help but notice he spoke, not in absolutes, but in terms of possibility. My previous display shamed me, but though I would not apologize for it, neither could I quite meet his eyes.

"You cannot know how it is," I said softly, straining to control the pain behind the words, "to be nothing, no one. You can't begin to understand how much of one's life—one's *worth*—is composed of nothing more than memories. Elastic, you call them. Unreliable, you say. Enhanced by imagination, perhaps. I may be deceiving myself. Maybe the things I think I'm remembering are not memories at all, and maybe believing that I can recover what I've lost is as foolish as grasping at fog. But when fog is all there is . . ." I closed my eyes briefly, fighting the need to weep. "Fog is what you grasp for."

He was silent for a long time. "The mechanism of humanity

is an intricate and delicately contrived thing. There is no measure for how much the power of wanting can influence what is. But before anything can happen, whether it is recovering your memory or claiming a miracle, you have to know what it is you want."

Ah, that simple, was it? For I wanted both, desperately, and I knew it would take a miracle to reclaim what I had lost. What did I want? I wanted to sit dozing in a sunny garden with a book on my lap. I wanted to taste cherries. I wanted the sound of children's laughter and the smell of the air in the evening after a rain. I wanted four familiar walls and a familiar bed, and to know I was where I belonged. I wanted answers.

Yet how odd it was that, until that very moment, I had never guessed how much courage it would take to set my foot firmly on the path toward claiming all those things. I was safe here. Nothing was demanded of me here. Even Michael, as frustrating as he so often was, required little of me, showed me small challenges. The world outside was a vast and uncharted territory, fraught with shadows and secret terrors, and I would be all alone. There might be monsters there.

There might be friends.

I turned to Michael, and looked at him steadily. "My name," I said, "is Mary. And I want to go home."

TWO

The trouble with people, observed the dog, is that they spend so much time making sounds they never get a chance to hear.

— *THE BOY WHO COULD SPEAK DOG,* PAUL MASON

To break the silence, Andrew said again, "This is the life." He nudged his deck chair around a little, as though for a better view, but what he really wanted a view of was anything except the kitchen window, and the two women who were visible inside the house through it.

With his beer bottle, he gestured to the wooded lot and careless wildflower garden that surrounded them, the glinting remnants of sunset on the blue-black lake below, the grill that smoked teriyaki chicken beside them on the stone patio, the squirrels playing tag on the bird feeder at the edge of the yard. "The small-town America we thought was lost forever, but leave it to you to find it intact. Yes, sir, you have got it made."

Every time he said it, Paul wondered who Andrew was trying to convince, himself or Paul. And he wondered, with detachment that felt more like weariness, what it was that made him try so hard at all. But when Andrew tilted his bottle

15

toward Paul in a small salute before he drank from it, Paul smiled and did likewise.

"Yeah," he agreed, also not for the first time, "I think this is going to work out fine."

He knew he probably should check the chicken, but for the same reason Andrew had moved his chair, Paul did not want to go to the grill. The kitchen window. One woman crying. Another comforting her. And a hundred feet away, two men who pretended not to notice.

"Of course," he said, "I've got a lot of work to do to get it ready for winter."

Andrew nodded. "Plenty of time, though."

"Landscaping, too, eventually."

"Sure, eventually. You going to try to put in central heat?"

"The contractor said there wasn't enough room to run the ductwork, not and keep the upstairs bedroom."

"What's that, Elsie's room?"

He knew it was. He'd had the tour. But Paul nodded, and took another sip of his beer. "You know girls that age. They need their privacy."

"So how is she liking it here?"

Paul shrugged, an elaborate display of casualness, and repeated, "You know girls that age."

Silence again. Birds sang and rustled in the trees overhead, and the sounds they could not hear from the kitchen were like thunder.

Andrew said, "So what are you going to do?"

Paul was startled. "About what?"

"Heat." Quickly, almost apologetically.

Paul sipped his beer. Like it didn't matter. "Space heaters, propane. That's the most efficient, in a house like this."

"Sure. Of course, you'll need insulation."

"The biggest part of the job."

"You're going to do it yourself?"

"What I can."

"Be glad to give you a hand some weekend. Just call."

Paul looked at him a moment, because he couldn't help it, and then quickly away. He said, "Sure." But this time when he sipped the beer it tasted like dust.

The silence ground on, probably no more than a few heartbeats, but between the two of them it seemed like hours. Out of the corner of his eye, Paul could see Andrew staring at the neck of his beer bottle. When he spoke he seemed to direct the words to the bottle, and not to Paul.

"It's not all that big a deal, you know." Quietly now, straining for neutral. "They cut it out, a few rounds of chemo, I'll be good as new. Not like I haven't been there before."

Paul's throat actually hurt with the words he wasn't saying. Words he didn't know how to say, and words that Andrew didn't want to hear. What he said instead was, "Hey, you bet." And he added, "But you know, in the meantime, if you or Cat need anything . . ." It wasn't enough. Not nearly enough.

"Yeah, I know." Spoken too quickly. "Thanks."

He tried again, desperately. "What I mean is, you know we're there for you, man. I mean, even if we are all the way the hell out in east Egypt, Cat's my sister, and you . . . Well, whatever you need."

"Right." The word wasn't as sharp as an exclamation mark, but it was definitely firmer than a period. Subject closed. Right.

Awkwardness settled around them like something clammy and fetid. Andrew Kirkhaven, head of the English department at the Woodlands Methodist College. Paul Mason, moderately acclaimed author of children's books and former professor at the same college. Educated, articulate, erudite; both the very epitome of the modern civilized male. Reduced to grunts and gestures around the campfire while their wives wept and held each other in the kitchen. A metaphor, Paul decided, for men and women since the beginning of time.

"Yeah," Andrew said after a significant pause. His tone had less feeling this time. "You've really got it made." He looked around, absently drank from the bottle. "Quiet. Good place to write."

"Yeah." If it weren't for Elsie and her dark silences, if it weren't for the hammering echo of his own disjointed thoughts, if it weren't for Penny trying not to look reproachful when she happened into his office and found him playing hearts on the computer . . . If it weren't for the serenity and the chaos, the quiet and the noise, the night and the day and the ceaselessly empty pages, this would be the perfect place to write.

Andrew glanced at him. "I mean, if you wanted to."

Paul said, not looking at him, "I put in an application with the school system. They've got four openings at the high school next fall."

Paul couldn't tell, in the deepening twilight, whether what he glimpsed of Andrew's expression was surprise or relief. "Well. Well, that's fine. That's good. You put me down as a reference, didn't you?" A half beat of silence, as though in quick debate; then the hurried reassurance, "Not that there's anything on your record—I promised there wouldn't be—but still, it might be better if they called me."

Paul cleared his throat. "Actually, I was wondering if . . . thinking it might be good if you could give me a letter, write something out, you know, for me to have."

There it was again, wrapped in silence as loud as a slap, all they couldn't talk about. A little thing called cancer, a girl by the name of Terri York, and you don't mind putting it in writing, do you old friend, because by the time the school system gets around to calling you for a reference you might be dead?

But Andrew just smiled. Looking tired and old and cancer-ridden, he said, "Be glad to. Might take a couple of weeks, though. I've got some stuff coming up."

"No problem. You'll bring it next time you come."

Then Andrew looked at him. "Maybe I'll just drop it in the mail."

The patio door slid open behind them and Penny called out, "Are you boys going to let that chicken burn?"

Her voice was filled with false cheer and just a trace of a low-country accent, and the sound of it sent relief washing through Paul that was more mellowing than any beer. The women were back. The crying was over. The lines of communication, such as they were, were reestablished.

He called back, "On the job, babe!" and got up, stopping by the cooler on his way to the grill. "Want another?" He lifted another brown bottle out of the melting ice.

Penny added, "Better light the torches too. Cathy says she's not bringing her world-famous potato salad out there to feed to the mosquitoes."

Andrew managed a grin that almost looked genuine, and answered Paul, "Sure. Why not?"

So they drank beer in the torchlight, and talked about yard work and fishing trips. When the girls came out they ate slightly blackened chicken and potato salad and lemon meringue pie, and Cathy even managed to coax a few sullen words out of Elsie. All in all, Paul thought, it was as much as he could ask for, and probably more than he deserved.

*   *   *

PAUL MASON HAD FALLEN in love with Penny Jarvis two days after he'd married her. She was a long-legged, golden-skinned brunette with flashes of copper in her unruly mop of curls that had always made Paul wonder whether she colored her hair to match her name or whether her parents had named her for the highlights in her hair. He had never asked, though. She had a funny smile and a wicked wit, and she was so damn smart it made his teeth ache, sometimes, just trying to keep up with her. He loved the nights of passionate academic debate, the way the sunrise surprised them sometimes when they realized all they had done was talk. He loved the nights of passion. He loved days spent looking forward to being with her; he loved the flash of her smile and the sound of her voice; he loved being a couple when she was the other half. But he did not know what it was to be in love with her until he married her.

Up until that point, theirs had been the perfect, almost clichéd romance: lovers throughout college, a backpacking tour of Europe after graduation, a long-distance love affair while he completed his masters at Columbia and she her internship at Duke. The only impulsive thing they had ever done was decide to marry in the middle of her residency, before he had even completed his Ph.D.

They did it in a wedding chapel decorated with yellow roses. She wore white lace and orange blossoms and asked his sister, Cathy, her best friend, to be a bridesmaid. They had three days for a honeymoon before she had to report back to the hospital, and they went rafting on the Nantahalla. Days were filled with river spray and salt sweat, nights with wood-smoke and musk. Sex in the wilderness. The sounds of cicadas and animals in rut. Life and love at their most exhilarating, and most elemental.

On the second full day of rafting—the first having been spent setting up camp and making love—there was an accident. They were both class-five-qualified rafters, and confident in their abilities. But the river was as unforgiving as it was unpredictable, and they were not prepared for the force of cascading rapids that spun the rafts around like a child's toy under a bathtub faucet, that snapped off one paddle against a rock, that swamped the raft not once but twice. And when Paul emerged from the second dumping, gasping, sputtering, and oddly exhilarated, Penny was not there.

He would never know another eternity like the one that he spent searching the foaming water with desperate, darting eyes, his lungs burning, heart slamming, throat raw. Suddenly everything was *real*: the ice-blue sky, the sputtering foam, the roar of the water, the empty, empty dip and surge and crash and break. Empty, cold, starkly absent of her.

He screamed. Maybe he screamed her name; maybe he simply screamed, loud and terrified and primal. *Penny. Don't die, Penny; don't leave me here alone. Penny. Don't be gone; don't make me live this life without you, Penny, Penny. . . .*

Searching, gasping, shaking, freezing, struck to the soul with the sudden, horrifying sense of aloneness. *Alone.* Was there any more bitter word in all of human language?

And suddenly she emerged, bobbing to the surface like a cork, choking and coughing and flailing like a puppy, her hair plastered darkly to her skull, her lips blue, her eyes terrified. Reaching for him.

He almost capsized the raft dragging her in, and he would have abandoned it entirely in another moment. This was hysteria; this was panic. This was what all the manuals cautioned you against, but the manuals didn't mean shit when the person you loved was involved.

She collapsed on the bottom of the raft, her teeth chattering, her arms linked in a death grip around his waist. There was a three-inch gash on her thigh, just below the hem of her khaki shorts, and as her body temperature warmed, the blood began to trickle, then to flow. He stared at the blood, the peculiar geometric pattern it made, and he thought, *This is mine. I am responsible for this. This is my wife; this is my wound. This is all my life, all I care about in the world.*

And he fell in love with her.

Penny still had the scar on her thigh, so faint it was almost imaginary most of the time. But when a summer tan deepened her skin to bronze the scar took on a pale pink hue, and Paul would trace it with his fingertip and be filled once again, as he had been on that day in the raft, with awe. *This is mine. I am responsible for this.*

Almost twenty years later he had fallen in lust with another long-legged, golden-skinned, bright-eyed girl, and for the briefest space of most intense fantasy, he had managed to pretend it was love. It was not, of course. Love was a pale pink scar on a leg that had seen seventeen summers of rafting and hiking, that had marched against apartheid and for a cure for breast cancer, that had knelt to tie shoelaces and wipe runny noses and had stood for ten hours at an operating table, saving a child's life. *This is my wife, all I care about in the world.*

But for the first time, loving her was not enough. Perhaps it never would be again.

THEY DID THE DISHES after Cathy and Andrew had gone, working with the easy rhythm of two who had performed the chore hundreds of times before. Paul rinsed and Penny loaded the dishwasher, and their conversation, though perfunctory, would not have seemed strained to anyone overhearing.

"Andrew looked good," Paul said. And added after a moment, "He seemed okay with things."

"He's not going to be okay, Paul," Penny said quietly. "Once a cancer of this type recurs, there's a twelve percent survival rate."

"Christ," Paul said.

"Right." She closed and locked the dishwasher. It gushed noisily.

He wanted to say more, but couldn't seem to think of anything appropriate. Death was just one more barrier between them. She dealt with it every day. He didn't.

She dried her hands and he waited to turn off the kitchen light. "I'll be staying in town tomorrow night," she said. "Seven-thirty surgery Monday morning."

He said, "I didn't know you were going in tomorrow. I thought you had the whole weekend." Trying hard not to sound accusatory.

"I do have the whole weekend." Trying not to remind him how hard she was trying, nor how long the commute to Chapel Hill was. "I won't have to leave until four or so."

All right. Okay. Adjust.

He turned off the light as they left the kitchen, and he slipped his arm around her shoulders, giving her a little squeeze. "Your loss, sweetie. Sunday night I make my famous fried catfish and Jamaican tartar sauce. That stuff doesn't keep, you know."

She laughed a little, and didn't try to shrug away. But neither did she lean into him. "And just exactly where were you planning to get these famous catfish to fry?"

"Off the end of my fishing pole, of course. I thought we'd take the boat out in the morning, see what we can catch."

"Better plan on ordering pizza for dinner. I've been fishing with you, remember?"

It was a nice moment, almost like it should have been. And then he said, "I'll ignore that. But all things considered, and since it's just going to be Elsie and me, maybe pizza isn't a bad idea."

"Actually," she said, too casually, "I thought I'd see if Elsie wanted to come to town with me. Maybe see a movie, go to the mall, you know the things girls like to do."

Oh, yes. See the friends she'd left behind—because of him. Do the things she could no longer do—because of him. Just another little reminder that all of their lives were diminished, because of him.

And just another way of saying that the summer was only a trial, they were merely visitors in his life, and it all could be taken away from him in a heartbeat. A single misstep, a badly chosen word, another failure on his part, and the house in Chapel Hill was waiting. For them, but not for him.

He dropped his arm from around her shoulders, tried to keep his tone neutral. "She's doing better here. You don't have to—" He broke off, swallowing words.

"Have to what?"

"Make it harder."

That was a mistake, as it usually was when he said what he thought. He saw the frost come over her eyes.

"I'm not trying to make it harder. God knows it's hard enough already."

He let a few moments pass, watching the regret for her hasty response shadow her face, fighting his own battle with sharp retorts that came too easily these days, to both of them.

At last he said, "Am I going to be paying for this forever, Penny?"

She crossed the living room, turned off a lamp.

"Because it's okay if I am. I just need to know."

She hesitated with her back to him, her shoulders tightening a bit, and she looked as though she might turn and reply. But she didn't.

He followed her across the hall to the newly renovated master suite—a gift to her, a bribe to make her come to him—and she went into the prettily wallpapered dressing room to change, speaking to him from behind the shelter of its walls. "We need to talk about Elsie."

He sat on the bed to remove his shoes. "We need to talk about a lot of things."

"Don't start this, Paul."

"What? And spoil a perfect evening?"

He hated himself for that. And for the silence that followed from behind the walls.

In a moment she came out, wearing a knee-length white sleep tee and ankle socks, brushing her hair. Her expression was stiff, held together with will and determination. She said, "We need to decide what we're going to do about school this fall. This disruption in the routine—"

"Disruption in the routine? Is that what we're calling it now?" He tossed his shoe toward the open door of his closet but missed, or maybe he threw it harder than he intended, because it crashed against the wall hard enough to make Penny flinch. Paul felt a stab of satisfaction, and he hated himself for that, too.

"For God's sake, Paul, there's no need to get hostile. And keep your voice down. It's after ten."

"I know what time it is." He flung his other shoe away and got to his feet, pulling his T-shirt over his head. "Do we really have to do this now?"

"Mike says—"

"Oh, of course Mike says!" He balled up his T-shirt and walked to the dressing room, where he stuffed it in the hamper. "I should have known."

"He thinks it's time we started reintroducing some structure into her environment."

"I disagree. I think that would only make things worse."

"How can you disagree?" There was exasperation in her tone now, and she was the one who was raising her voice. "We're paying him thousands of dollars a month for his expert opinion!"

Paul came out of the dressing room in his pajama bottoms. He never used to wear pajamas. Now he did. Everything changed.

He said, "I disagree because I'm her father and her teacher, and I spend more time with her than both you and Mike Turner combined. Is that a good enough reason?"

He knew he had gone too far when he saw the flash of vulnerability in her eyes, followed almost instantaneously by the tightening of the muscles of her jaw, a defense against hurt. He took one apologetic step toward her but it was too late. The wall was up.

She said, "I told Mike we'd start preparing her for public school this fall."

Paul started at her. "You did what?"

"Paul, it's time. We can't keep putting this off—"

"You should have asked me. We should have discussed this."

"I am asking. We are discussing."

He tried to keep his voice reasonable, but without much success. "It doesn't sound that way to me. It sounds as though you've decided, and you're informing me."

"Look," Penny said tightly, "do you at least agree it can't do any harm to talk to her about it?"

"No, I don't agree!" He was shouting and he couldn't help it. "I think I've made it clear that I think this is completely unnecessary. Besides that, it could do a lot of damage—"

And Penny interrupted coolly, "Really? More damage than what has already been done?"

The blade drove home and twisted. They held each other's eyes for a moment, wounded and wounder, waiting, although neither one of them could have said exactly what they were waiting for. And then the brittle silence was broken by the sound of hasty footsteps racing up the stairs, and a slamming door.

Paul went out into the hallway and looked up the stairs. Elsie's door was shut tight. He started to go to her, and then his eye was caught by a glint of something out of place in the parlor. He went into the moonlit room and crossed to the window. He saw the broken lamp at the same time that he felt a stab of pain in the ball of his bare foot. He cursed softly and jumped back, balancing on one foot as he pried the small piece of glass out of his foot.

"Damn," he said, and the sentiment was not for his injury but for the pieces of antique cobalt that were scattered across the board floor. He remembered the day Penny had found the lamp at a junk store on a Virginia highway. It must have been a hundred and ten degrees inside that shop, but she wouldn't leave until she had searched every cardboard box and dusty shelf in the place. She came up with a 1912 edition of *Huckleberry Finn* and a tarnished silver and blue lamp, which she had insisted in triumphant whispers was genuine cobalt. She paid fifteen dollars for both items, and they left the store chortling over their luck. Afterward they had ice-cream cones at a scenic overlook and laughed about how they'd have to buy a table for the lamp, and then a chair for the table, and then a rug for the chair. It had been a good day.

Now it was shattered.

He hobbled back to the bedroom, trying not to track blood on the floor.

"What happened?" Penny was on her feet.

"Stepped on a piece of glass. It's okay." He sat on the edge of the bed and plucked some tissues from the box, pressing them against his foot.

She brought a washcloth from the bathroom. "Let me see."

"It was the cobalt lamp in front of the window."

Her hand paused in its ministrations with the tiny cut, but only for a moment. "I didn't hear anything."

"It might have happened earlier."

"Elsie?"

"I'll talk to her in the morning."

"I guess she heard us."

"I guess."

Penny turned back to his foot. "I don't see any glass."

"I think I got it all. I'll get a Band-Aid."

He took the faintly bloodstained washcloth to the bathroom and rinsed it out, put a bandage on his foot. When he returned she was getting into bed.

He said, "I'm sorry about the lamp."

"It's not your fault."

"I know you liked it."

Her face was tight now, completely closed to him. "It was just a lamp."

She turned off the light.

They lay in silence for awhile. Then she said, softly, "I hate it when we fight."

It was one of those moments that, if he had known how to capture it, how to use it, might have changed everything, or at least something. There was something he could have done, something he could have said, that would have made a difference, he was certain of it. But all he could find to say was, "Me, too."

He leaned over and kissed her on the cheek, but it seemed like a hollow thing. They lay for a long time in silence side by side in the king-sized bed, not touching, listening to the sound of the lake lapping softly against the dock, lost in their own sad and separate thoughts.

THREE

How to describe my homecoming? Wondrous, breathtaking, exhilarating . . . tragic, lonely, disappointing. Beyond the weighted gate, which was badly in need of paint, across the cracked stepping stones, to the yellow house which, in the fading light and to my tired eyes, seemed rather a dingy shade of beige. It was all as I remembered it . . . and nothing was.

Someone had prepared the place for my arrival. The floors were polished, the furniture dusted; fresh flowers from the garden spilled from a blue-and-white vase on the table in the small foyer. Signs of such thoughtfulness brought a lump to my throat, and I wondered what kind neighbor or friend I had to thank for the gesture. But did it matter? Someone cared for me. Someone wanted me to be comfortable when I returned home. I wasn't alone, and I tried to fortify myself with that.

I wandered through the house, touching unfamiliar objects, searching, listening, aching for something that I recognized. In the kitchen I was startled when I twisted a handle and water sprayed from the faucet. I couldn't figure out how to work the stove. I wanted to cry.

I don't know what I had expected. Everything that I loved, everything that I knew, had been wiped away at the same time my memory had. There was no voice to call me "darling," no small, plump arms reaching up for a hug, no happy spaniel racing across the lawn in pursuit of a rabbit . . . those things that made a home, those things that cried welcome, they were gone. This was just a house, the dusty bones of something once alive, and the emptiness that filled me with that understanding was so enormous I thought it would suck me dry, and I, like the collection of memories I once had been, would simply shrivel up and blow away in the wind.

I knew Michael was waiting for me just outside the gate, gentle in his understanding and strong in his certainty. I was not ready for this. He would take me back where I belonged.

I moved deeper into the house.

I passed the pretty cherry-wood staircase and paused there uncertainly. Upstairs, a bed awaited me. A bed I had shared with a husband I could not remember, a bed with a white counterpane set beneath an open window. Would it be wood or metal? Carved or painted? Or would it be there at all?

I moved past the staircase, and into a room with a fireplace and many windows, comfortable furniture covered in faded prints, pretty rugs on the floor. Perhaps I recognized it; perhaps it only seemed welcoming. I liked the room. I felt comfortable there. And I was drawn, as if by the whisper of unseen voices, to the mantelpiece, and the row of photographs arranged there.

I drew in the first breath it seemed I had taken since I awoke in the sanitarium. And wonder, cautious and liquid, flowed through me like warm honey.

The man in the photograph had curly sandy hair and

squinty laugh lines around his eyes. A slightly oval jawline and a kind mouth. I knew that face, that hair, those sun-lined eyes. It was absolutely familiar to me.

My husband's name was Jeff. He liked fishing, reading Milton, and walking with the dogs on November mornings. When he chopped wood for the winter fireplace he would come inside smelling like white oak and man—sweat and wool damp from the mist—and I wanted to bottle the fragrance and save it for empty days and long evenings when his patients took him away from me. His name was Jeff, and he was well loved.

I caressed the photograph, drinking in the image. This one face I knew, this flood of memory suddenly rising at my feet, this gave me life; this gave me strength. There were more pictures of him: raising a string of fish and laughing into the camera, standing on the prow of a small sailing boat, bundled in winter clothing beside an enormous snowman. And though I didn't remember the moments, the face, the blessed familiarity of the face, entranced me. It filled me with hope, and it broke my heart.

My eyes darted from one photograph to the other in unabashed greed, not tasting but gobbling them, not savoring but inhaling them. The familiarity of that face was my anchor, and the details were irrelevant. And then I stopped, and all the world around me went still.

The photograph showed him holding a child, a little girl of about three, with a mop of curly dark hair and his mischievous smile. My daughter?

And there she was at five, casting a triumphant look at the camera from astride a bicycle. And there she was, oh, so pretty in a white dress, sitting in a white wicker chair with her dark hair curling around her shoulders. And now she was older, standing in front of a house with a woman I didn't recognize, and there she was with her father again, Daddy's little girl, on a fishing trip, my baby, my daughter, my child, and there was no recognition in me at all, just an overwhelming sense of guilt and loss.

I lifted my hand toward a photograph of a baby girl in a white dress and white lace cap, wanting to hold it, to clutch it to my breast and rock it to me as I must have once rocked the child whose image it preserved. But the grief that filled me was monstrous and thick; it sucked my energy and my will and left me only sorrow, bleak and dark.

I stumbled to the sofa and collapsed there, curled up into a ball with my arms hugged to my chest, too weak to even weep.

"Oh, Michael," I whispered, aching in every fiber. "I had a child. And I think I killed her."

"WHY DO YOU THINK THAT?" Michael asked calmly.

Of course a condition of my release was that I should return to see him periodically, and discuss the problems I was having. It was my safety net. I was not alone. I could come back to this safe place anytime I wanted, and they would take care of me.

Maybe he had been right all along. Maybe I wasn't ready to go home. But I wasn't ready to admit that.

So I told him my problems—but not all of them. I didn't tell him how I had grown so frustrated over my inability to work the table lamp that I had finally thrown the thing against a wall in a rage. Nor how the shrilling of the telephone had terrified me the first time I heard it, nor how I was still unable to use the cookstove. I didn't tell him about the ladies who had come to call and how awkward it had been, not knowing who they were nor what to say to them, and how we had sat on the sofa for an interminable half hour while they talked about things I didn't understand until I finally made some pathetic excuse and fled the room. It was humiliating.

I didn't tell him how weak I felt, how overwhelmed, and how all I wanted to do was sleep, all the time. But I think he knew.

I replied wearily, "I think I must have always known it, on some level. I am here; they are not. When I look at the pictures, I feel such horror, such helplessness . . . it's my fault they died. And I think that's what I am trying to forget."

He nodded thoughtfully. "And you tried so hard to forget their deaths that you also forgot their lives, as well as your own."

"It has happened," I replied a little sharply. It seemed to me he should be the one reaching these conclusions, not I.

Again he nodded. "Guilt is not a particularly helpful emotion, however, is it, when you can't remember what it is you're guilty about?"

"My family is dead!" I cried. "I saved myself but my family is dead and it's all my fault!"

He gave me a small half smile. "You must be a powerful person, to hold mastery over life and death."

I replied stiffly, "I was a mother. And a wife." I was responsible. It was self-explanatory.

He was silent for a moment, no doubt considering my words. Then he said, "So you postulate that your amnesia stems from the guilt you feel over your family's death. The question would be then, I suppose, What are you going to do about it?"

I stared at him. "What an absurd question. They're gone. There's nothing I can do about it."

"No?" The surprise in his voice was feigned, I'm sure.

"How odd. Guilt usually presupposes the opportunity for atonement. If there is no atonement—nothing you can do about it—perhaps the guilt you feel is not the appropriate emotion at all."

I found him to be, at that moment, the most annoying creature I had ever met.

I stood abruptly. "I have to go home."

"Why?"

Ah, another one of his pointedly pointless questions. It made me agitated. "There are things I have to do."

I thought he would try to stop me, or ply me with more ridiculous questions. But all he said, after another moment's gentle pause, was, "When you have figured out what those things are, I hope we can talk again."

My relief was so enormous I was only too ready to agree.

I had almost made good my escape when he said, "Mary."

I hesitated.

"The bed."

Now I was confused. "Bed?"

"Was it metal or wooden? Painted or carved?"

I felt a stab of panic because the truth was, I didn't know. In all the time I had been home I could not remember once having gone upstairs, although of course I must have done so. I must have slept in that bed every night, but . . . I couldn't remember.

I lifted my chin. "It's metal," I said. "Painted white."

He smiled at me, and nodded, and I think he knew that I was lying. But he was, at least on that occasion, kind enough to say nothing.

I WENT IMMEDIATELY up the stairs and into the bedroom. White shutters were drawn against the late-afternoon sun, casting prison bars of light on the polished oak floor. A paddle fan turned lazily, shadow and light, light and shadow. There was a mirrored vanity, and fresh flowers—not daffodils after all, but peonies—on the dresser. It all seemed so strange to me, familiar yet strange, just slightly out of synch. My room . . . yet not.

My heart hardly seemed to beat nor my lungs to breathe as I turned toward the bed. The bed was made with a fluffy feather mattress and a wedding-ring quilt worked in pale blue and rose. There was a stuffed bear with a tattered blue bow propped up against the pillows, and a felt mouse dressed in blue gingham, with a white pinafore apron and a mobcap. The bed itself had a high wooden headboard carved with garlands, and it was painted pale yellow.

Defeat drained me of energy and left me numb. I drifted to the bed and sank down upon it, and I was asleep before I felt the touch of the pillow against my cheek.

I had the strangest dream. In it there were voices, and at first they were simply murmurs, blurred sounds like the hums of a dozen different bees which gradually separated into distinct babbling sounds which then, much to my surprise, became words, and those words belonged to different voices.

Male: *You should have asked me. We should have discussed this.* He sounded angry, and as though he was trying not to be.

Female, reasonably: *I am asking. We are discussing.*

Male: *It doesn't sound that way to me. It sounds as though you've decided, and you're informing me.*

Female: *Look, do you at least agree it can't do any harm to talk to her about it?*

Male: *No, I don't agree! I think I've made it clear that I think this is completely unnecessary. Besides that, it could do a lot of damage—*

Female, coolly: *Really? More damage than what has already been done?*

Silence like a thunderclap, and then the sound of a door shutting, loudly. Loudly enough to wake me up.

I sat up in bed, groggy and disoriented, reflecting over the peculiar clarity of the dream and wondering if I had in fact dreamed it at all, or whether the neighbors might have left their windows open, allowing me to eavesdrop unintentionally on a private marital discussion. But the nearest neighbors were around the bend and shielded by a sturdy stand of oak trees; this I knew clearly. I could not possibly have overheard anything coming from their house.

Puzzled, I swung my feet to the floor and started to rise. And I was frozen in place.

The room was in twilight, the sun having sunk deeper below the horizon while I slept and the shutters remaining closed. But the door to the hallway was open and the lamps in the hall were lit. Had I done that before falling asleep? I couldn't remember. But there was light spilling in through the doorway to the bedroom—that part of the doorway, that is, that wasn't blocked by a figure.

I gasped and clutched foolishly at the bedcovers, as though for protection. "I beg your pardon!" I cried, thinking that some neighbor or unknown friend, having tried to rouse me by ringing the bell below, had become worried and let herself in. Alarmed, trying not to be. "I . . . Who are you?"

But she did not answer. She simply moved into the room as though she had every right to be there, barely glancing at me, and shut the door hard behind her. It was then that I realized the figure was that of a young girl, no more than fourteen, surely, rather plump and sloppily dressed, with tangled dark curls and angry eyes. She marched over to the window and opened the shutters and stood there for a moment, slouched against the casing with arms folded, gazing out toward the dusky distant mountains, scowling so fiercely that I knew the scowl could conceal nothing but tears.

The last rays of day were pink and orange, tinged with purple; not light so much as mood. Yet it was light enough for me to see every detail clearly. The shoulder-length curls, so carelessly caught back at the neck, the flushed face, the determined jaw . . . I recognized that face. I recognized it from more than a photograph on a mantel. I recognized it with a mother's heart.

"Sarah," I whispered, for no other reason than that the word had welled out of me like water from a deep spring. Not a word. A name. The name of my daughter.

Then I cried, "Sarah!" And I scrambled across the bed, tangling myself in the covers, tripping and nearly falling as I lunged across the floor toward the window, arms open, hands grasping.

But when I reached her, my hands closed on nothing but air. She was gone.

A dream, you say. The voices, the apparition, nothing more than tangled memories, the mind trying to make a wish come true. I thought so too, for a while. But as the days went on, and I looked back to that afternoon, I realize that was the moment when I first began to understand that I was not alone, after all.

My house was haunted.

FOUR

The boy figured he couldn't be all that stupid, if someone
as smart as the dog looked up to him.

—*THE BOY WHO COULD SPEAK DOG*, PAUL MASON

FROM THE DIARY OF ELSIE MASON

*They were arguing about the psychiatrist, if you can believe
that. They don't say* psychiatrist *of course; they say* counselor, *like they were talking about freakin' Deanna Troy from
the starship* Enterprise *or something. Yeah, right. They're up
all night fighting in tight little whispers they think I can't
hear (Bulletin, parents, dear: it's so quiet in this godforsaken
place you can hear a rabbit fart ten miles across the lake), she
practically breaks a lamp over his head, and the next morning
there they are pretending like nothing ever happened, and they
think* I'm *the one who needs counseling? Well, forget it. I
don't care how big a hunk this Dr. Turner is supposed to be
(this from my dear friend Sarabeth, thank you very much, you
bitch, because my mother never would have thought of it—she's
way too busy to even notice me, much less think about what I*

do or do not need these days). If her mother hadn't been raving about how good Dr. Turner had been for Jill—if only she knew, ha, ha. Now, there is one screwed-up cookie, and her friends too, half of them crazy on E and the other half just crazy, and I don't even know why I like her, and sometimes I don't, but, hell, I guess everybody has to have a best friend and this is the one I get. Like I said, ha, ha. Anyway, it's all a big waste of time. What do they expect me to tell him, anyway? How much I hate this place? No TV, no video, not even any air-conditioning, if you can believe that! And the bugs! I mean, yeah, OK, it was fun for a few weeks in the summer when I was a kid, but who wants to live here? I can't believe he wants us to actually live here! And what is it with him that he thinks he can make everything OK by just striding in in the morning with that big shit-eating grin on his face and saying, "Let's go for a ride on the boat!" I don't even like the boat. It messes up my hair, and God knows I don't need any more freckles on my face, and it's going to take a lot more than a day out with Dad to get me in a swimsuit, I'll tell you that.

Besides, to go on the boat I'd have to go to the boathouse, now, wouldn't I?

They probably think I hate them. I don't. I know they're just human, and they do stupid things, and I guess I'm disappointed in them, and that makes me sad. But I don't hate them. What I hate is my life.

And this place. I really hate this creepy place. I even think it might be haunted. But I'm not telling Dr. Hunk Turner that. Then they'll really think I'm crazy. Ha.

"Holy Christ! Goddamn it!"
Elsie clattered down the stairs and into the kitchen in time

to see her father holding his hand under a stream of cold water at the sink. Even from a distance she could see the reddened palm, and his face was a grimace of pain. "Damn it, Elsie, did you forget to turn the stove off again?"

She looked at him coolly for a moment before replying, "I haven't used the stove all week."

"Well, somebody did. You girls have got to be more careful! You could have burned the house down."

She went to the freezer, scooped up a couple of ice cubes, wrapped them in a paper towel, and brought them to him. A flash of thanks warred with the pain in his eyes as he accepted the ice cubes, and applied them gingerly to his wounded palm. "I guess your mother left it on when she made her tea this morning," he grumbled in a moment. "She was in a hurry to leave."

Elsie muttered, "Can't blame her there."

"What?"

"Maybe you're the one who left the stove on. Everything's not always our fault, you know."

He seemed to catch a retort before it was spoken—something he was getting quite good at these days—and glanced down at his hand. He rubbed the melting ice cubes across it one more time and tossed them in the sink. "Sorry I snapped at you," he said. The corner of his mouth worked its way into a wry little smile. "First the lamp, and now this. If I were given to paranoia I'd think someone was out to get me."

Her eyes were sharp and defensive. "I told you I didn't break that lamp."

He looked at her for a moment, seeming to debate. Then he said, still smiling, "Guess it was the wind."

Elsie turned to go upstairs.

"Elsie, wait just a minute, will you?"

She turned, but kept her expression stony.

He pulled out a chair at the table, gesturing her to sit, and she ignored him. He turned his eyes toward the window with its view of rolling lawn and the lake beyond, as though searching for inspiration. He said, "Remember the summer I taught you to dive off the dock? We were going to surprise your mom; then she came up early for the weekend and just about killed us both because she thought it was too dangerous." He turned back to her ruefully. "It was, too."

"Is there a point?"

"Not really. I was just wondering if maybe you'd like to go swimming later."

"You have got to be kidding. That water is like fifty degrees."

"It's not that bad."

"Besides, I don't like the water."

He was incredulous. "Since when?"

"Since now." She scowled. "Can I go now?"

He said, "We used to walk in the woods and look for fairies, remember? You had names for all of them."

"Jeez, Dad, that's lame. I'm thirteen years old, for Christ sake."

He sighed and looked at her straight on. "I'm trying real hard, honey. I want us to be a family again more than anything in the world. I know we're not going to walk in the woods looking for fairies. I know you're too old to think diving off the dock with your dad is cool. But I am trying like hell to put this thing together again, and if there's something I'm supposed to be doing that I'm not doing, I wish you'd just tell me, because I'm out of ideas."

She hadn't expected him to say that. She was angry to be

caught off guard, and at the same time she suddenly loved him so much, and hated him so much, that she felt tears spring to her eyes. And she hated that more than anything.

She wanted to spin and run up to her room and slam the door and lock it, but that was exactly what a thirteen-year-old girl who was unable to cope with family stresses would be expected to do. So she swallowed her hot, wet emotion and she said, "Maybe some things can't be put back together again. Maybe some things are just broken."

He just looked at her without accusation or regret. "Like the lamp."

"Christ." She turned in disgust to go.

"Let me ask you something."

If she had really wanted to go, she would have kept right on marching. But that was the thing. She didn't really want to go. She wanted to hear what he was going to say next.

He said, "Last year, when it was just you and me, doing your lessons four times a week—did you like that?"

She shrugged. "It was okay. It was fine."

"We used to talk about things, Elsie. Not just schoolwork, but lots of things."

She shrugged again.

"I used to think there was nothing we couldn't talk about."

She said, "Guess you were wrong."

That one scored. She could tell he was trying to hide it, but the hurt in his eyes was just quick enough for her to see. She should have felt triumphant. She felt rotten.

He went over to the stove and turned off the burner on the stove, his back to her. "Your mother thinks we should reconsider your school arrangements."

Elsie felt an irritating need to make up for her stinging

remark of a moment ago, to continue the conversation with him. "Well, that's her job, isn't it? Reconsidering things."

"She'll want to talk to you about it."

"She knows where to find me."

But that seemed like an awkward exit line, so she cast about for something else to say.

"So where is the great Earth Mother, anyway? Off saving the world again?"

"It's not as though she repairs televisions for a living, you know. She repairs human bodies. Her work is important, Elsie."

"I thought we were important. Don't I remember some family meeting somewhere when we all agreed that this summer our family was going to be the most important thing? Isn't that how we all ended up out here in the middle of nowhere doing the Swiss Family Robinson thing?"

He hesitated for a moment; then he looked at her. "You're right," he said. "We did."

When she was a little kid, she used to love that look. The look he'd give her when she had been smart enough to come up with a point he could not dispute, when she was right and he was honest enough to admit it, when she used the grown-up rules to win the game. But now the look was tinged with sadness and defeat, and she found the last thing she wanted was to be right.

She scowled. "I don't know what you expected, anyway. We have lives, you know. We can't just drop everything for a whole summer."

He forced a half smile as he bent to pick up the sponge he had dropped when he burned his hand. "I thought that was the point. Change of scenery, chance to get away and reevaluate. Besides, you used to like coming here."

She fixed him with a glare. "Aren't we over what *used* to be, yet? I used to like the lake. I used to believe in fairies. Besides, there's a difference between vacationing here and living here."

He avoided her eyes. "Nothing has been decided yet."

And the double meaning behind *that* was probably the saddest thing of all. It made her throat tight again. She said, "Well, you'll be sure to let me know when it is, won't you?"

She spun around and started out of the room, quickly, before he could see her chin quivering, and then she heard it again: voices, laughter, a child's playful squeal, but muted, as though the sounds were coming from the room on the other side of the wall. But she could see the room on the other side of the wall, she had just walked through that room, and there was no one there. And then, as abruptly as if someone had turned off a radio, the noises stopped.

She whipped her head around to look at her father, to see if he was listening too. But he was sponging off the counters, shoulders tired, jawline tense, and gave no sign of having heard anything at all.

She said hesitantly, "Daddy, do you ever . . ."

He looked at her with such quick hope that she wanted to bite her tongue. She hadn't called him Daddy since he had left them in March. Childish, maybe, but it was the best she could do.

"Do I ever what?" he prompted.

"Nothing," she said, indescribably irritated with herself, and she left the room, stamping her feet hard on the stairs, as though to shake the dust of might-have-beens from her feet.

The first time it happened was in broad daylight. Dad was locked away in his room, writing—or pretending to, more like it—and Mom was supposed to be at work, so when I heard this woman's voice you can bet I went sneaking down quick to see who was back there with him. Only as soon as I hit the bottom of the stairs I realized the voice was coming from the kitchen, and other sounds too—like dishes, and water running, and she was saying ". . . even hotter today. If we've got enough ice maybe we'll make ice cream after supper. I've got some nice strawberries put up. . . ." By that time I was in the kitchen and there were all these sounds, like people moving and dishes being put away, and she went on chattering about strawberries for maybe thirty seconds or so, and there was absolutely no one there. Then gradually the sounds kind of faded away, like a satellite moving out of range, you know, until there was nothing at all.

Sometimes I hear a grandfather clock chiming, and we don't have a chiming clock. There are other little sounds, like silverware rattling in the dining room, like someone's setting the table, or footsteps on the stairs, or a porch swing creaking—and we don't have a porch swing either. But mostly it's the voices. Just regular voices, saying regular stuff. Nothing important. I mean, not like they're telling me to go out and pull a Columbine or anything—now, that would be what you might call important—but just family stuff, like Don't forget to put your shirts in the basket because today is laundry day, and If you add a little white vinegar to the water, the windows won't streak when you wash them. (Now, I ask you, how could I make that up? Why would I even want to?) It's like, if you could punch a little hole through into someone else's life, and catch random pieces of conversation as they happened by, this is what you would get.

Or maybe it's a hole in time. Maybe the voices are the

sounds of all the people who have ever lived here before, little snippets of memory trapped inside the walls of this house by some kind of weird space-time anomaly. Maybe they're just plain old-fashioned ghosts.

See, that's the major difference between my parents and me, and why I can't even tell them about the voices, even though I really am curious whether they've heard them too. I believe in lots of things. And, as far as I can tell, they don't believe in anything at all.

FIVE

I think everything began to change the day I went to the garden.

After all those days of longing for my garden when I was locked away from it, I had not had the strength to go there once in all the time I had been home. But on that morning I stood at the window with warm summer breezes billowing the lace curtains and bringing with them the dancing scents of wild rose and honeysuckle, and I thought, *Today I will go to the garden.*

If the honeysuckle weren't cut back regularly it would take over the fence, and the wild roses had a tendency to twine themselves around the blackberry vines to make a thicket that would be impenetrable come blackberry-picking time.

I smiled at the thought of a July kitchen, standing over a kettle thick with simmering juice, swollen jelly bags dripping the steaming nectar, face hot, armpits dripping sweat down my sides and dampening my waist, stirring the concoction with a long-handled spoon, testing it by drops in cold water until it jelled just right. Burning my fingers on hot jars fresh from a boiling water bath, pouring melted paraffin atop the hot jelly to seal it perfectly around the edges.

And the smell . . . ah, the thick, sweet steamy smell of blackberry jelly, big kettles of it, cooked all day, how it clung to the curtains and seeped into the cushions, and seemed to settle like a taste on the back of the tongue into the very walls themselves so that sometimes, even in the depths of winter, one could catch a whiff of that scent and be instantly transported back to a hot July day when all the world smelled like blackberries.

It was a memory so rich, so complete, so delightfully vibrant, that I sighed out loud with the sheer loveliness of it.

I went out onto the porch, reaching automatically for the garden hat I always kept hanging on a peg by the door. It wasn't there, and annoyance flickered through me, which I quickly squelched, for it was too fine a day, too rich with memories and the possibility of memory, to be spoiled by the things I couldn't remember. Like where I put my hat.

Or how long it had been since the last time I had hung my hat upon that peg.

I went out into the garden with my small basket of tools upon my arm, and for a moment simply stood there, comforted by the feel of the sun on my shoulders, the familiar creak and snick of the ball-and-chain gate latch as it closed behind me, the shrill *cherie, cherie* call of a bird overhead. Had I ever known the name of that bird with its sweet, distinctive song? It suddenly seemed a great adventure to learn again all the things I had forgotten, or perhaps had never known, and for the first time I looked into the future and felt like smiling.

I turned then, half glancing back over my shoulder as I

rounded the house toward the cutting beds, and the oddest thing happened. My vision blurred, as though from sleep or tears, veiling everything with a shimmering distortion. I blinked rapidly to clear my eyes and when I looked again my house— my pretty little yellow house with its wraparound porch—was different. It was only an instant, but it was a shocking sensation, to look and see what is familiar, to look again, and see that familiar thing changed. The porch was longer, wider. The cobbled path was covered by grass. The tin roof was painted red and there were more windows. The color was not as yellow as it once had been, yet brighter somehow, crisper. There were other changes, I'm certain, but it was all so fast that these, the most obvious, were all I could catalog. I caught my breath and took a half step back and in the blink of an eye all was as it had been before.

A trick of lighting, I told myself, a mirage composed of shadows and moving air. But my heart was tripping in my chest and I dared not admit what I knew to be true: it wasn't the morning light, it wasn't the motion of shadows. It was a mind that was broken beyond repair, and that had not yet begun to reveal all the ways in which it could not be trusted.

I hurried, then, around the house toward the rose beds, abandoning my idea of weeding the perennials, which might not, after all, be where I remembered them. And that was when I got my second shock.

The roses weren't there. In my absence someone had ripped them up and burned the clippings, for there was not so much as a thorn to remind me of the lush, fragrant garden this once had been. Or perhaps one thing: the stone bench, rough-hewn and pitted with time, where I used to sit in the twilight and watch the colors fade, was still there, shaded by a poplar tree so tall that all the ground was littered and moist with generations of its dropped leaves. Roses would never grow here, I thought, holding on to the edges of reason by my fingernails. It was far too shady. Why had I ever thought roses would grow here?

And yet how well I remembered sitting here in the cool of the evening, a soft shawl draped over my shoulders, listening to the water, watching the fireflies, inhaling attar of roses. I walked over to the bench; I touched it. Yes, it was here. I sat, hesitantly at first, half expecting it to disappear beneath me. But no, it was as solid as time, as certain as my memory of it. Perhaps, during my long illness, the roses had become blighted and died, and a conscientious gardener had dug them up. That was possible.

But where was my frog?

I turned around on the bench, searching the landscape slowly, deliberately. I could picture it exactly in my mind, a twelve-inch-high frog carved of granite, squatting whimsically with its mouth open to trap any unsuspecting fly that happened by. It had sat in its spot beside the bench so long that its front feet had become imbedded in the ground, and its back had grown covered with moss, which gave it an absurdly realistic appearance. Why would anyone move my frog?

And suddenly I was angry. I felt as though my home had been invaded, my treasures and my memories casually swept aside, my entire life cavalierly rearranged for the convenience of strangers. I was a blind person whose markers had been taken away, and I was left to speculate and calculate my way through an increasingly treacherous landscape. It was not my memory that had failed me; it was my world. And that made me angry.

I stood up and began to search my surroundings with ever-increasing frustration, kicking at the weeds and vines that encroached upon the bench, pacing off angry steps around the tree. Perhaps it was not the frog that had been moved, but the bench. I tore up clumps of creeping vetch and tossed them away, I swept back piles of leaves with my foot, and when I spied an uneven spot in the earth I fell to my knees and began to dig, clawing away clumps of grass and dirt with my fingers. I felt stone and tugged at it but it wouldn't loosen. I dug away more dirt; I pried and rocked at the stone. I wedged my fingers in deeper, excavating earth and enlarging the hole, until at last I was able to ease the stone free.

I held in my hand a blackened lump of granite about the size of my fist, much too small to be my frog. Still, I pried out dirt from the crevices, I rubbed the stone with my palm, I knocked away chunks of debris, and gradually a shape began to form. And my heart began to pound.

I held in my hand the head of my stone frog. Its stone eyes were still bulging; its stone mouth was still open. But scars had been gouged from its face, as though with a heavy blade, and it was sliced clean through at the neck. Decapitated.

The horror I felt was completely out of proportion to the discovery, and I couldn't say why. My heart stuttered and went loud in my chest, my breath was tight, and there was a sick, hollow feeling in my core. It was only a frog. Only a stone carving that once had guarded a garden bench, not even a very good carving, inanimate, unimportant. And yet as I knelt there, covered in earth, holding its remnants in my hand, I felt my very world rock, subtly and inexplicably, upon its axis.

I can't say how long I sat on the ground, breathing hard, staring at the shadow of my past. Surely not as long as it appeared. For when I finally let the heavy granite head roll to the ground and braced my hands against my knees in preparation for rising, I realized the shadows had grown long, the day faded. I got to my feet, absently rubbing the earth from my hands, feeling empty and disoriented. And then I saw her.

She was standing only a few feet away, half-lost in the shadows of the oak, staring at me. Dark hair framed her face and wreathed her head like a soft, puffy cloud, and her eyes were faintly luminous, like the last coals on an ashen hearth. Her expression was still, suspended like a held breath, and intent upon me. As I saw her, I felt my own breath catch, and my hand fluttered to my throat. Before I could stop myself, I whispered, "Sarah?"

It was a question, for suddenly I was no longer as sure as I once had been that the revenant I was seeing was the grown-up version of the photograph on the mantel, my own beloved daughter.

She made no move, gave no sign that she had heard me. I took an almost involuntary step forward, my hand extended. "Sarah, is that you? Who are you? Please answer me."

She began to back away, moving farther into the shadow of the tree, and my heart leapt to my throat. "No! Wait, please, don't go!"

I rushed toward her, but of course, by the time I reached the place she had been, she had disappeared.

I made a small, frustrated sound beneath my breath, and turned back toward the house. That was when I caught a glimpse of something—a flash of movement, a flutter of clothing—just rounding the corner. I began to run.

Stumbling a little, I rounded the corner of the house, but there was no sign of the girl. I paused to catch my breath, looking this way and that, and that was when I noticed a light from inside the house. That was curious, since I certainly had left no lights burning when I had left for the garden that morning. Now dusk was approaching, and yellow light cast a pool upon the close-cropped grass outside the kitchen window. I moved close.

Even before I reached the window, I caught a glimpse of movement inside. I felt a catch in my heartbeat, and I proceeded cautiously, picking my way between the clumps of wild iris, trying to stay close to the wall. I peered hesitantly inside.

She was there, my darling girl, moving around my kitchen as though she had always done so, opening a cupboard, reaching for something, moving to a table set for two. And then he appeared. Sandy haired, crinkle eyed, gentle faced, the man in the photographs, the one so familiar to me, so close in my memory I almost could wrap my hand around it and call it mine.

"Jeff," I whispered, and I could hardly make a sound for the leaping, pressing, choking rhythm of my heart. I lifted a shaking hand to the windowpane and pressed it there. "Jeff!"

He moved across my range of vision, disappeared for a moment, and before I could strain to follow him, returned again with a blue enamel pitcher, which he set on the table. He smiled at the girl, and said something to her I could not hear. She put a big bowl of greens on the table, and moved out of my sight.

I cried, "Jeff! Sarah!" and I pounded my open fist briefly on the window. They didn't hear me, and I cried again, "Jeff! I'm here! Look at me, look!"

He turned, instead, toward the door, and moved toward it.

Heart racing, breath choking, I ran toward the back door. Did I expect to see them there, my lost family? Of course I did. They had lied to me at the hospital, or Michael was mistaken. They weren't dead after all, my baby girl and my beloved husband. They had aged, but so had I. They weren't dead. They were here; they were waiting for me!

Breathless, stumbling, choking on tears of exhilaration and delight, I flung open the door—to a kitchen that was dim with the shadows of twilight, cold as stone, and completely empty.

SIX

The only difference between then and now, according to
the dog, was what time they served dinner.
—*THE BOY WHO COULD SPEAK DOG,* PAUL MASON

It had become a habit over the past year for Penny and Cathy
to meet for a late lunch in the café across the street from Dr.
Turner's office while Elsie was in her session. These days it was
one of the few times either of them ever got to relax and be
herself.

Penny and Cathy had been roommates in college, and it
had been on a holiday visit to Cathy's home that Penny had
met Paul, and had fallen in love with him almost the same day.
Paul used to tease her that the only reason she married him was
to have Cathy as a real sister, and Penny used to tease him back
that there was a lot of truth in that.

Ten years later, at a Christmas party given by Paul and
Penny, Cathy met Andrew Kirkhaven, thirty years her senior
and head of the English department at the college where Paul
held what they all called his "play job." Six months later Cathy
and Andrew were married, and less than five years later he was

diagnosed with cancer in one of his kidneys. The affected organ was removed, he responded well to chemotherapy, Cathy went back to work at the research department of the university library, and Andrew missed less than six weeks from work all told. Now the cancer had made another appearance, in his liver this time. After three more weeks of radiation therapy he would undergo surgery.

But they did not talk about that. That was not what these lunches were for. They didn't talk about Elsie either, or Paul, any more than they had to. For an hour or so each week, they were girls again, best friends and roommates, and the things they talked about they would share with no one but each other.

"Jesus, kiddo," Cathy greeted her, breezing Penny's cheek with a kiss before sliding into the banquette seat opposite her. "You look as bad as I do. Maybe we should skip lunch and go straight to the cosmetics counter."

Penny grimaced. "It'll take more than a complete makeover to repair the damage, I'm afraid."

"How about a week at the spa?"

"Make it a month, and who's buying?"

"You're the big-shot surgeon. I'm just a lowly librarian with a mortgage."

"I'll call your mortgage and raise you a freshly remodeled lake house and an unemployed husband."

"My heart breaks."

They looked at each other, half smiling, without accusation or irony. Penny reached across the table and squeezed Cathy's hand. "Are you sleeping okay?"

She shrugged. "I've got some Valium."

Penny leaned back, hiding a yawn with both hands. "Maybe I should try that."

The waitress came and they both ordered coffee, black, and shared a weak grin as they did so. They took a ritual moment to glance at their menus, but they each knew what they would have. Penny, chicken salad and fruit. Cathy, tuna on rye. The point of their lunches, they used to joke, was not the lunch, but the dessert. Now they knew the point of their lunches had very little to do with food whatsoever.

They put their menus aside and Cathy said, "How can anyone have trouble sleeping in that incredible place? The lake lapping against the shore, the crickets singing their little hearts out, the breeze rustling through the trees . . . I would think the problem would be staying awake."

"Maybe that's it. All those crickets and lapping lakes, nothing but racket all night long."

"And?"

Penny hesitated, and shrugged uncomfortably. "And nothing. It's just these weird dreams . . ." But she shook her head dismissively. "The commute is a killer. I'm probably just overtired, and I worry all night long about all the things I didn't get done while I was in town."

"The commute is not going to get any easier if you decide to stay."

The waitress brought their coffee and they gave their orders. Penny concentrated on stirring artificial sweetener into her cup while Cathy waited for an answer to the question she had not asked.

Penny said, "I've cut back on my practice. Maybe not as much as I'd hoped to . . ." *As I said I would,* she corrected herself honestly. "But I'm not taking any new patients—except the ones the hospital sends me when I'm on call, of course— but I do have a partnership to report to, not to mention the fact that people are depending on me." Hollow arguments, even to her own ears. She sighed. "Truth is, it's just not that easy to cut my ties to the city." She looked down into her coffee, tracing the circular ripples her spoon made in reflections of dark and light. "Truth is," she added softly, "I'm not sure how badly I want to."

Cathy nodded, understanding. "Any chance you could all move back to the city?"

"Not anytime soon," Penny said. "Paul was right about that, anyway. Too many memories, all of them bad. On the other hand, I don't see how we can *not*. Not if I'm going to keep up my practice."

"Paul told Andrew he was hoping to teach at the local high school this fall."

Penny shifted her gaze over Cathy's shoulder. The subject made her uncomfortable; the death of dreams always did. "I wouldn't mind, if that was what he really wanted to do."

"I think he really wants to."

"He's better than that and you know it."

Cathy smiled. "Yeah, I know it. Glad to hear you still do, too. What kind of dreams?"

Penny was too accustomed to her friend's thought patterns to be surprised by the change of subject. "Creepy dreams. Bloody dreams. Not fit for the lunch table."

"You cut into people all day long," observed Cathy pragmatically. "At night you're supposed to dream about kittens and butterflies?"

But Penny couldn't force a smile. The mere mention of the dreams had brought a chill to her skin and a slight tightening to her throat. The dreams belonged at the lake. Here, she was safe.

The thought startled her, and she looked at Cathy, trying to put her feelings into words. "It's like . . . the house turned on me. Isn't that a funny thing to say? Like houses have personalities, or wills. But that's what it feels like."

"But you love that house!"

Penny nodded. "It used to be my safe place. Now . . . I guess no place is safe."

Cathy said gently, "I know that feeling."

And because one of the rules of their luncheons was "no guilt, no pity," Penny just smiled wanly and answered, "I know you do."

They talked about random things over their salad and sandwich, and made an elaborate production over choosing the dessert they would share. They were both in better spirits by the time they decided on a banana bread pudding served with caramel rum sauce, vanilla bean ice cream, and chopped toasted walnuts, as they always were by the end of one of their lunches. They ordered more coffee with the dessert and then Cathy said, "Oh, I almost forgot! Paul will get a kick out of this. You'll never believe what my genealogy research turned up."

Cathy had been tracing the family tree, with all its various branches and offshoots, for five years now. Penny did not find the whole thing terribly interesting, but because Cathy was her friend she pretended to.

"There's no telling," she said. "Skeletons in the closet, I hope. That's always exciting. Especially if someone you know put them there."

Cathy made a face. "Well, sorry to disappoint you—no skeletons precisely, but how about a family scandal? It turns out that one of our ancestors—Paul's and mine—was accused of being a Yankee sympathizer during the Civil War and run out of town on a rail."

"Lord preserve us!" Penny clapped a hand over her heart and fell back against her chair. Cathy ignored her happily.

"He was a music teacher, son of a dentist. . . ."

"And probably gay."

"Penny!"

"Just trying to liven up things a little."

"Well, this *is* lively if you'd just let me finish. For a while it looked as though that branch of the family had disappeared, or died out with him, but then I started casting a wider net, and you'll never guess."

"He and his transvestite wife turned up in a commune in California."

"And to think I ever complained about your lack of imagination. No, Ms. Wise Guy, it looks as though the exiled traitor might actually have settled in the Lost Villages area—right where you guys are living now!"

Penny frowned a little. "Lost Villages" was the term some of the locals used to refer to the three adjoining villages— whose names she could never remember when she needed to— that had been partially destroyed when the lake was built in the thirties. She hadn't heard the phrase in a long time, and she noticed for the first time what a haunting, lonely term it was.

She said, "That seems unlikely. I mean, Paul and I stumbled on the whole area by accident. How weird would it be if it turned out one of his ancestors actually lived there?"

"You know what Jung said—there are no coincidences."

"I think that was Freud."

"Whoever."

"Anyway, I would think a thing like that would be pretty hard to prove. I mean, most of the records must be underwater for what?—seventy years?"

"Actually, there's quite a bit of information available on the area. You just have to know where to look."

The dessert arrived and they spent several moments exclaiming and moaning in admiration before picking up their spoons. Then Penny said, "So are you going to look?"

Cathy glanced up with a spoonful of ice cream halfway to her mouth. "Sure. I mean, why not?"

Penny twirled her spoon in caramel sauce, her attention focused on catching the drips. In a voice only slightly too casual, she said, "Let me know if you find out anything about our house."

"Like what?"

Penny could feel Cathy's eyes on her. "I don't know. Anything."

"Anything like what?"

Penny scooped up a spoonful of bananas and nuts. "Like nothing. Forget it."

Cathy looked as though she wanted to pursue the matter, but Penny toasted her with her spoon and a big smile, and challenged her to a race to the middle of the monstrous dessert. They finished their lunch with laughter and happy gossip, and for a while Penny was able to forget how much she dreaded going home.

AT SOME TIME during the day Elsie decided she would just do it. She would walk down to the boathouse and just look around, not even go in but stand on the outside and look. Maybe she would open the door. Maybe she would stand there until her eyes adjusted to the dark and maybe she would take a step inside, just one foot on the narrow ledge that hung over the deepest cover in the lake, and maybe then she would see what was making the noise. She knew in her head it was the anchor ropes moaning against their moorings, or maybe the hull whispering against the dock. But sometimes it sounded like voices.

She could hear the music before she came downstairs; her dad was in his so-called office with the Beatles on CD, leaning back in his chair and looking at nothing, tapping a pencil on the edge of the desk in time to the music. She paused at the door for a moment but he didn't notice her.

"Genius at work," she muttered, and moved on. The music was too loud for him to hear her, but she wouldn't have cared if he had.

She was crossing the front hall when something caught the corner of her eye. It was a person, she was sure of it, moving past the set of double windows in what her mother called the parlor. Not just a person. A woman. Her heart began to beat a little faster because she knew who it was.

She cast a quick, uncertain look back at her father's office, not even sure why she did, and then she hurried out the front door.

Elsie had seen her first from the window of her room as she looked down upon the backyard. It was sunset, and she was just standing there, looking out over the lake like any tourist—only she was in *their* backyard, and she wasn't a tourist.

She had actually reported it to her parents that time— "Hey, Dad, there's somebody wandering down around the lake." But he hadn't found anyone when he went to check. She had forgotten about it until, a few days later, she had come downstairs to get something to eat and had seen the woman— or at least she *thought* she had—going into the parlor. When she looked no one was there.

The third time she and her mom were coming back from

town, and there she was, as big as life, sitting on the front porch swing, fanning herself with what might have been a folded magazine. She had exclaimed, "Hey who is—" and stopped herself when her mother drove right past the porch—too close *not* to see someone sitting on the swing—and said nothing but "Who is what, hon?"

When Elsie twisted her head around to look again, the swing was empty.

And then she started thinking about the voices, those strange, out-of-sync muffled radio transmissions from someplace unknown into their twenty-first-century kitchen, and decided that the next time she saw the woman, she was not going to get away so easily.

Most people would have declared "Ghosts!" of course. But Elsie had more imagination than that.

So she left the house quickly, careful not to bang the screen door and alert her father, and she hurried toward the back of the house, following the direction in which the woman appeared to have been heading. She rounded the corner of the porch and she stopped still, hardly able to believe it.

There she was, not ten feet in front of her, a woman in a gingham dress and dark hair, real and solid. And weird.

Weird because of the way she looked, in some indefinable way, something about her hair or her dress or the way she carried herself that seemed out of place and out of time. And weird because she was, in fact, wandering through someone else's property with a flower basket, just as though she was out for morning work in the garden—someone else's garden. But mostly weird because when Elsie called out she didn't even turn her head.

"Hey!" Elsie called again, and moved closer, even though

there was no way the woman could have not heard her at that distance. "Hello! Can I help you?"

The woman put down her basket and stood for a moment beneath the shade of a big poplar. She turned her head this way and that, as though looking for something. She looked straight at Elsie, a sun-scowl on her face and nothing more, and her eyes moved on as though the girl standing in the path were nothing more than a tree or a bush.

Elsie came closer, moving slightly more hesitantly now. Something was weird. Definitely. "Uh, this is private property, you know."

She did not appear to hear, but turned instead and sat on the stone bench beneath the tree, looking irritated and preoccupied.

Elsie was no more than six feet away. She could see the woman's face clearly, a face that was neither beautiful nor plain, brows that weren't very well shaped, faint sharp lines on her forehead and around her eyes that suggested she either frowned a lot or laughed a lot, or spent time outside without her sunglasses. She might have been thirty, but would have looked younger with makeup.

Elsie said softly, "You don't look crazy. But you sure act it."

The woman did not seem to hear Elsie at all. Or see her.

Cautiously, Elsie took another step closer. "Do you have a name?"

And Elsie sprang back with a gasp as the woman suddenly lunged to her feet and began to look around wildly. Elsie backed up so quickly that she fell into a hydrangea bush, righted herself, took a few scrambling steps, and tripped over a stump, landing hard on one knee.

By the time she got to her feet again and dusted off her

jeans, the woman was on her knees on the ground, digging frantically in the dirt with her bare hands. Elsie stood still, not daring to move, and watched until the woman pried something out of the dirt and sank back, cradling it in her hands.

A quick, excited thought of buried treasure flashed across her mind—it was, after all, possible—but faded into disappointed curiosity as she took a step closer. "What *is* that?" she said.

The woman turned when she spoke, and her eyes went wide when they fell on Elsie. The object she was holding tumbled to the ground as she got to her feet. Instinctively Elsie took a step backward.

The woman's lips formed an oval, as though she were saying something, but no sound came out. Elsie moved another step backward and the woman stretched out a hand. More words. No sound. Elsie moved farther back, and alarm crossed the woman's face; she lunged for Elsie.

Elsie couldn't help it. Like the girl player in a B horror movie who always gets it in the end, she turned and ran.

She was almost to the lake before she ran out of breath, and when she collapsed against a tree, gasping, she was no longer being pursued. Still, she stayed there, breathing hard and searching the landscape until she was sure she was alone, and then she slowly climbed the hill back to the house.

She went first to the poplar tree, approaching cautiously. She even picked up a stick on her way to use as a club, and she didn't feel a bit foolish for brandishing it. When she reached the bench where the woman had sat, there was of course no one there.

But the earth beneath the tree where the woman had dug was still turned, leaves and debris scattered. Moving as though she were negotiating an ice slick, Elsie moved close, and carefully picked up the dirt-encrusted rock the woman had dropped. She waited. Nothing happened. She looked around. No one was there.

She turned to go inside.

HER DAD WAS IN THE KITCHEN, a Scotch in his hand, looking rather aimlessly through the cabinets. He glanced at her and said, "Wash that thing off outside. Your mother will kill you if you track that dirt through the kitchen."

She said, "Jesus, Dad, drinking this time of day? Are you turning into an alkie now? That's so cliché."

"It's after six. And I can't believe I just defended my drinking habits to a thirteen-year-old." Almost defiantly he took a sip of Scotch.

Elsie stared in mild disbelief at the clock in the breakfast nook. It couldn't be that late. It had been lunchtime when she left the house, and she had been gone only a few minutes.

Weird, she thought.

"Do you feel like anything special for dinner? It's going to be just the two of us."

"Surprise," she muttered, but with something less than her usual venom. Then she said, "Hey, Dad, who was that guy that wrote all that stuff about relativity and time travel?"

He stopped his aimless search through the cabinets and looked at her in surprise. "You mean Einstein?"

"Yeah, him. Do you suppose they have any of his books in the library?"

"You mean the local library?"

"Oh, yeah, the one that doesn't exist." Already she was feeling uncomfortable for having asked. "Forget it."

"Why the sudden interest?"

She shrugged. "You know. They're talking all the time about quarks and wormholes and temporal distortions on *Star Trek*."

"OK," he said, eyebrow lifted. "I'm raising a kid who knows about quarks and wormholes but who never heard of Einstein. I believe we could spend a little more time on the physical sciences next year."

"Whatever." She crossed the kitchen toward the hall.

"You know I'll be happy to take you to the university library whenever you want."

"Jeez, Dad, don't suck up about it."

"How about not talking to your father that way?"

His tone was so sharp it actually stung, and she stopped, not certain whether to be angry or hurt. The best she could do was try to hurt back, so she said, "Mom can take me to the university anytime I want to go."

"So she can."

He wouldn't look at her, but stood gazing out the window, sipping his drink. His jaw was knotted, and she thought she might really have touched a nerve. That should have pleased her, but it didn't.

And even though what she really wanted to do was stalk away, she heard herself saying, "Let me ask you something."

He turned to her with a look of polite question on his face, and distance in his eyes. She knew that look. She had seen him give it to her mother often enough.

She plunged recklessly ahead. "So what would you call it if you heard voices having conversations when no one was there, and saw people who disappeared when you got close?"

He frowned a little. "Are you telling me you hear voices?"

"Oh, for Christ sake, Dad, you're so literal! We were talking about *Star Trek*, remember? Temporal distortions?"

The frown only deepened, but she thought it reflected more impatience than confusion. "Well, they may call it temporal distortion on *Star Trek*, but in the real world when a person hears voices and sees things that aren't there we call it schizophrenia."

"Great, Dad, just great!" She would have thrown up her hands in exasperation if they had not been weighed down by the heavy stone artifact, so she shrugged her shoulders elaborately instead as she spun away. "No wonder you haven't written a book in ten years. You have absolutely no imagination!"

A shocked silence followed her exit, and she felt kind of bad about it until he shouted after her, "Eight years!"

She clattered up the stairs.

"And come back down here and help with dinner!"

She slammed her door.

FROM THE MOMENT they first had seen it, Penny had loved the house. The yard was overgrown with weeds, the fence was sagging, ivy had cracked the chimney and completely covered one side of the house, and the siding was rotten in more places than it was intact. Inside, the floors had been covered with a horrible gray linoleum, which was now cracked and peeling, and the paint—most of which was blistering or flaking off—was lead based. But all she had to do was squint her eyes and she could see through the ravages of time into the gorgeous Victorian bones of the structure beneath.

Paul had wanted to drive right past, but she had practically tumbled out of the car before it stopped, in her eagerness to explore. She was enchanted by the wraparound porch with its delicate turned columns and gingerbread trim, by the little cottage garden fence, by the green plantation shutters. She did not notice that the porch was gray with weather damage and some of the trim was little more than sawdust and glue held together with cobwebs, that the fence was missing pickets, or that the shutters were sagging and gap-toothed. And when they walked around back even Paul had to admit that the view alone was worth the price.

So they got a key and walked through, talking about how easy it would be to rewire, since all of the electrical wiring was on the outside of the walls anyway, and what a mess it would be to pull up the linoleum and strip the floors, and how much they loved the big bathroom—which had obviously once been a bedroom—and the claw-foot tub. They had lunch at the diner half a mile away, and talked about how they really couldn't afford a second home with a baby coming, and what a steal the asking price was even if it would cost a fortune to renovate, and how much fun it would be to spend their weekends remodeling the house of their dreams. They stopped by the real estate office to turn in the key and ended up signing a contract.

By the time Elsie was born, Paul had eliminated the lead-paint hazard and stripped the floors down to their bare oak finish. Penny had bought lace curtains and chintz sheets and hand-stitched quilts, and piece by lovingly selected piece, had begun to fill the rooms with flea market finds. The pictures of their first summer there were of plaster dust and sunsets over the lake, and in every single one of them they were laughing.

Elsie learned to walk on the soft grass carpet of the back-yard, and Paul extended the fence to encircle both the cottage garden and the backyard, and installed safety latches to keep the baby away from the lake. With his first royalty check from *The Boy Who Could Speak Dog*, Paul had put in a dock, and in the first year Penny earned a six-figure income, they bought a boat.

Wallpaper came down; wallpaper went up. An antique candlestick here, a reproduction armoire there. Bright white paint for the porch, restorations made on the shutters. Finally, as Elsie grew older, they had sacrificed the one big bathroom for two, and Penny had loved every change, every sweaty hour spent with paintbrush or scrub brush, every bent nail she had hammered and every crooked screw. The house had become part of the family; loving it, nurturing it, and watching it grow had become part of the fabric of their lives, binding Paul and her together in the same way that Elsie did.

And now she was afraid to come home.

It had begun only days after she and Elsie had moved in with Paul for the summer. He had gone to so much trouble re-modeling the kitchen for her, a project they had stopped and started so many times over the years that she couldn't bear to tell him how much she hated it, that maybe the reason she had never been able to decide on a countertop was because she liked the old countertop, and he had no right to make such changes without her. She didn't say it because they had too many real and important things to be angry and hurt over, and because she knew that the remodeled kitchen was not really what she hated at all. But it made her uncomfortable every time she entered it. It didn't feel like home anymore. And it wasn't hers.

And so she came into the kitchen for coffee one morning, as she had done a hundred mornings before, and was struck by a sticky wetness on her bare feet. The morning was overcast, and there wasn't enough light coming through the window for her to see what she had stepped in, but she could see the source. A dark puddle was dripping from the counter onto the floor, like spilled syrup, and another puddle seemed to have formed behind the cabinet overhead. When she moved closer to the cabinet she saw that someone had been there before her, and left dirty handprints all over the white-painted cabinet, and the facings, and even the wall. She turned slowly and saw streaks of the stuff smearing her white lace curtains, and her tablecloth, and tracked across her shiny floor.

She turned back to the puddle on the counter, and touched her fingertip to it. She was a surgeon; she knew the feel and smell of blood. But she had to touch the stuff again, to bring up her whole palm shiny red, before she could believe it. And then, horrified, unable to stop herself, she reached up and opened the cabinet. A tidal wave of blood spilled out, splashing her nightgown, her face, getting into her eyes and her mouth, and she stumbled back, trying to wipe away the stains, but the more she scrubbed, the worse the stains became, until she was covered in it, sliding on the blood-slick floor, falling, and too terrified even to scream.

When she awoke, gasping and sweating, the taint of the dream was so intense, the feeling of it was so real, that she had to go stand under a hot shower for half an hour, and still she was afraid to go into the kitchen.

She did not need a psychiatrist to interpret the dream. Her kitchen had been massacred; her home was bleeding and broken; her marriage was mortally wounded. And she couldn't get the stain of it off her no matter how hard she tried.

And it wasn't getting any better. Instead of diminishing in intensity, the dreams were actually increasing in detail and drama. In the latest one, she had seen a baby's foot peeking out from behind a bloodied table leg, and from the angle and the stillness she had known the foot would never move again. Her baby, her Elsie. Not just her home, but her family, had been brutalized and destroyed. The dream had been so terrifying, so bleak and dreadful, that even now, two days later, it took all of the courage Penny possessed to get out of her car, cross the lawn to the back gate, and open the kitchen door.

There was no blood, of course. Nothing but a cozy, homey scene—Paul and Elsie, just sitting down to dinner with yellow Fiestaware on bright blue placemats and cobalt tumblers filled with iced tea. The vintage-look refrigerator hummed, the soapstone countertops gleamed, and there was no blood on the new slate floor. In her dreams, the kitchen was always as it had looked when they moved in.

There was a split second before they noticed her when Penny had one of those rare moments that were so sweet they should be captured in time, and could, in a single instant, erase all the unpleasantness that had been stored up before. Her husband, her daughter, so alike and so different, each of them and both of them caught between childhood and adulthood, beautiful and immortal. A quick unguarded moment when Elsie forgot to be angry and Paul forgot to be on the defensive and they were simply two people sitting down to dinner, reaching for the salad tongs, ladling up soup. Just two people whom Penny loved more than all the world.

"Mom!" Elsie said, and the surprise in her voice sounded almost like pleasure.

Paul's chair scraped as he turned quickly and stood up. "Honey, hi! We didn't think you could make it for dinner." He moved to gather up another place setting.

"I broke away early." She hardly had to feign the pleasure in her voice at all as she added, "Glad I did, too! What's that I smell? Blackberry pie?"

"Sorry." Remembering that pleasantness did not fit her current persona, Elsie leaned her chin in her hand and poked her fork around the lettuce leaves. "No one here knows how to cook. Soup and salad."

"Chef's salad and gazpacho," Paul corrected. "I used up the last of the tomatoes we got at the farm stand last weekend. Besides, it's too early for blackberries."

"Oh. I guess it is." She turned her cheek for the brush of his kiss as he passed, and tugged at one of Elsie's wild curls as she sat down. Elsie shrugged away and speared a forkful of salad.

Penny sat down and unfolded her napkin. Long ago she and Paul had made an agreement not to talk about their work at the dinner table, and it was an arrangement that had served them well for many years. These days, however, it left topics of conversation embarrassingly short. She tasted her soup; she resisted the urge to tell Elsie to stop playing with her food. In a moment she said, "Cathy came by today. We had lunch." And before Paul could ask the inane, "How is she doing?" Penny went on. "Did you know she was back to tracing your family history?"

Paul gave her a look that said he wasn't surprised. Cathy always had a project going, and the more stressful her life became, the more challenging the project was likely to be. "Oh, yeah?" he said, trying to be genial. "Let me guess—horse thieves and cardsharps, right?"

"Probably." Out of the corner of her eye Penny saw that Elsie actually seemed to be paying attention to the conversation, and she was pleased. "Also a tobacco farmer, a dentist, and a music teacher who had the very bad judgment to be a Yankee sympathizer during the Civil War. He was exiled from the family and never heard from again."

"Ha. I knew there was a scoundrel or two in there somewhere."

"Cathy thinks some of his people may have actually settled around here. Hard to trace, though, because that branch of the family seems to have died out in the thirties."

"Ah, well, wouldn't you know. The interesting ones never last long. Nothing but a bunch of lawyers and accountants in the family from then on, huh?"

"Pretty much."

"Why would they do that?" Elsie said.

It was so unusual to hear Elsie voluntarily contribute anything to the conversation that both parents stared at her for a moment. Then Paul said, "Do what?"

"Why would anyone settle around here?" she said somewhat petulantly. "There's nothing here. Not even a town. How would they even find it? I don't even know how *we* found it."

Paul said, "Well, you know we're only thirty miles from Logantown by the old road, which is where most of my family came from, at least on my dad's side. That's how your mom and I found this house in the first place, when we were coming back from my grandfather's funeral."

Elsie gave an expressive little snort and said, "Figures."

Penny added, choosing to ignore the rudeness and reward the interest, "Besides, this used to be a thriving community before they built the lake. There were a lot more houses, and stores, and a church and even a post office. You can still see the post office in the wintertime from the end of the road here. It's that little red building with the roof caved in and all the vines growing up the side. It even had a name. Do you remember what it was?"

She looked at Paul and he shook his head. "Something churchy. Bethel, Calvary, Redemption, something. I'll bet Cathy would know."

"She said she was going to do some research on the area. Maybe even our house."

"There might be some stuff in the attic she could use. Seems like I remember a box of old pictures and receipts and odds and ends like that." Paul glanced at Elsie. "That might be a project for you, kiddo, if you're interested."

Elsie shook her head with a pinch of her brows that was meant to look annoyed. "I'm not. God, a person can't even ask a simple question around here without getting assigned a project. May I be excused?"

Paul glanced at Penny, and then he said, "The three of us don't get to have dinner together very often. It would be nice if you could stay until we're all finished."

"Whatever." A word perfected by, if not invented for, thirteen-year-olds, which managed to convey in three short syllables disgust, disdain, disinterest in and disillusionment with the entire human race, and its adult components in particular. She rolled her eyes in punctuation and added, "Can I get a magazine, then?"

Penny said, "You're excused, Elsie."

"Great. Just in time to catch the Sting concert on Pay-Per-View. If we *had* Pay-Per-View, of course. If you need me I'll be up in my room, watching the spiders reproduce."

When she was gone Penny said in a low voice, "I wish you wouldn't make me the bad guy."

"I don't think it's too much to ask that a child have dinner with her parents once in a while. Especially when it *is* only once in a while."

Her lips tightened. "You knew that was the deal from the start. I have a practice that's three hours away—"

"Actually, I thought the deal was that you would cut back on your practice. I guess I didn't read the fine print."

Silence congealed between them, sticky and cold. Penny touched her napkin to her lips, pleated it absently with her fingers, and placed it beside her plate. She said, "I spoke to Mike Turner today. He likes the idea of a private school to start with."

She had lived with Paul too long, and knew him too well, not to read in his face all the things he was trying not to say. Finally it was, "I see."

He got up and began to clear the table.

"I told you I was going to talk to him about it," she reminded him.

He was at the sink, and he didn't turn around, but she saw his shoulders stiffen. Like she had driven a knife between them. "And I asked you not to."

She took her bowl and her salad plate, both of them barely touched, and set them on the counter beside the sink. "I told Mike you disagreed."

"Good of you to mention my opinion."

"You do sarcasm badly."

"I'll take that as a compliment."

"You could have talked to him yourself. It might be good if you did."

He looked at her. "I've told you from the beginning that I'd go with you to any marriage counselor you chose. I begged you to go to counseling with me last winter, if you recall. You weren't interested."

"I was more interested in saving my daughter than saving my marriage last winter," she replied. "I don't apologize for that."

"And now? You're telling me something has changed?"

"Damn it, Paul, it's not always about you! This just can't be about you right now, OK?"

He inhaled sharply, seemed to be about to say something else, then deliberately erased all emotion from his eyes and his tone. "Right," he said. "I'm the villain. You're the victim. Got it."

She turned to leave the room, and then stopped, drawing a long, deep breath. She looked back at him, and spoke with difficulty. "Don't you understand, Paul? It used to be that whenever I was scared I could talk to you, and things would seem a little better. I'm scared now, but there's no one to talk to. And that's the worst thing that's happened to us."

The anger left his eyes and was replaced with shadowed regret. "I'm scared, too, Penny. Maybe we could start by just saying the words. Just trying to tell each other what's wrong."

And it seemed in that moment, in that single fleeting instant, that it was almost possible, and the words tumbled up into her throat: *There's something wrong here, Paul; there's something wrong with this house, something we never knew before; there's blood in the kitchen and the walls are filled with awful memories, and I know it sounds crazy but I think they're trying to tell me something. . . .*

And even as she drew a breath, and almost choked on it, she knew that five years ago, perhaps even two, she could have said those words to him and he would have taken them as seriously as if she had said, more simply, more reasonably, *I'm afraid the family that I cherished but didn't take care of has been shattered forever and I'm afraid it's all my fault.* And she knew that as hard as she tried, she was incapable of saying either one of those things to him now.

She could not stop a weary, regretful smile from crossing her face, and she shook her head. "It's funny. It's such a small thing. And I know if I could do that, then everything would be all right. But I just can't."

"Penny." His voice was tired. "This isn't going to work, is it?"

The words stabbed her like icy needles in the center of her chest. She couldn't look at him, and she had to swallow before she could reply. "That's what I'm trying to find out," she said. "All I'm asking is . . . a chance to find out."

She left him alone and went upstairs.

When, Penny wondered, had it become against the rules of society for a parent to invade the sanctity of an offspring's room without knocking? She rarely thought about things like that unless she was in this house, when it seemed that the parents of four generations before looked down upon her in sad bemusement as she huddled outside the door of her teenage daughter, her hand poised timidly to knock, almost afraid to disturb the tentative peace.

Elsie grumbled a reply to her soft tap, and Penny entered the room. This had been the original master bedroom of the house, with a small nursery adjacent. Paul and Penny had remodeled the nursery into an additional bath and closet space, and turned the room over to Elise when they had added the new master bedroom downstairs with its French doors, private deck, and full view of the lake. Still, she missed this room sometimes. The sloping, uneven ceiling, the heart-pine floor with the scars of dozens of unknown feet, the way the light filtered in slowly in the morning, making lace picture patterns upon the floor, just as it had done for so many wives before her. There was a timelessness to this room, and she used to like to lie in bed in the mornings and imagine she had, in fact, been transported back in time, and that nothing awaited her but a dewy morning and blackberry vines heavy with fruit, a cow to be milked, a baby to be bathed, a porch upon which to sit and shell peas. But then, as likely as not, the phone would ring, or her pager would go off, or a motorboat would roar rudely across the cove, and it was the twenty-first century again.

Little had changed about the room since Elsie had moved in last year. No posters on the wall, no favorite photographs, not even a boom box. Elsie would stay here, but she wouldn't live here. It was a statement. Penny immediately went over to the one object on the dresser that seemed out of place, and picked it up.

"Good heavens, what's this? A gargoyle?" A scattering of dirt rained down when she turned it over, and she handled it more carefully.

Elsie was lying on her bed with her hands behind her head looking at nothing at all. She glanced at her mother, then away. "A frog head. I found it in the yard."

"Interesting." Penny replaced the object on the dresser, brushing at the crumbs of dirt that preceded it. "There's a market for antique statuary. It might be worth something."

Elsie shrugged.

Penny came over to the bed, lay down, and folded her hands behind her head. She let the silence lie as long as she could, and then she said, "I know you're not my baby anymore. But I love you anyway. Dad loves you too, and he does his best to let you know. It's just that guys that age are . . . awkward." The little joke fell flat. A year ago they would have been giggling and tickling each other by now.

Silence, silence, silence. It felt like a drumbeat.

Elsie said, "Aunt Cathy came by the hospital today?"

"Yes."

"For one of Uncle Andrew's treatments?"

Only a slight hesitation. "Yes."

"Uncle Andrew is going to die, isn't he?"

So flat, so matter-of-fact, so hopeless. A tone of voice that never was meant to belong to a thirteen-year-old child.

And Penny's hesitation this time was barely noticeable. "Yes," she said quietly. "I think so."

Elsie said nothing for a few breaths. Then, "Do you ever wonder why everything happens to us?"

Penny knew she should choose her words. She knew this was an opening, a chance to parlay conversation into something more meaningful; a chance, maybe, to take a step toward making them mother and daughter again. But she was too tired to be a parent tonight. She was too tired to do anything but gaze blankly at the ceiling and answer, "All the time."

In a moment she said, "Have you thought any about going back to school this fall?"

"What's the point?"

Penny turned her head to look at her daughter. "What do you mean?"

"I mean, who even knows where we'll be in three months? Here, or in town, or . . . who knows?"

Damn, Penny thought. *Damn, damn, damn . . .* But she said, "Actually, it would work out fine either way. Transferring to high school after being out a year will be a lot easier than if you were going back to middle school, and trying to pick up where you left off with your friends and school activities. I've been looking into Hidden Hills, that nice prep school over in Lakemont; remember we talked about it? It would only be twenty minutes away if—from here, and it sounds pretty cool. They even have a course in dressage! I thought we could go look at the campus next week if you want to."

"I don't ride horses."

"Well, I know, but I thought it would be fun to—"

"Anyway, I kind of like being home-schooled, and my scores are better than they were in public."

"Well, I know, but don't you miss going to school every day, seeing the teachers and the kids, and, well, doing things?"

Even before she said it Penny knew that was a stupid question. Elsie had never been very social, and her participation in school events was grudging at best. She had a few friends who were carefully chosen, and she saw them outside of school. She was not surprised when Elsie said flatly, "No."

"This was never meant to be a permanent situation, Elsie."

"Maybe it should be." Her voice was a little too deliberately casual. "The old man's a pretty good teacher, you know."

"I wish you wouldn't refer to your father that way. It makes me feel old."

"Sorry."

"And I know he's a good teacher. His students—" She had started to say, *His students loved him,* then realized what a sick double entendre that would be under the circumstances and, worse, how it would open her up to ridicule from her daughter. *I hate this, I hate this,* she thought, and every muscle in her body tensed as she said, "Maybe we should talk about this in a family meeting. I'm sure your father would have a lot to add."

"Great." Sarcasm now. "I love our family meetings."

Penny took a breath. "You should know I already discussed this with Dr. Turner. He agrees with me. Your dad doesn't."

"Gee, what a surprise."

Elsie sat up, her back to Penny. Penny sat up too. "What do you mean?"

"God, Mom, do you think I'm deaf, or stupid? I heard you arguing. And it's not as though I could exactly ignore the lamp you threw at him."

"I've never thrown a lamp at anyone."

"Oh, yeah? That pretty little porcelain one by the window? How did it get broken then?"

Penny said, "I thought you—" And then she stopped.

Elsie made a disgusted face. "Jeez, Mom, do I have to take the blame for everything around here?"

"No one blamed you."

"And that's even worse! You wouldn't even *talk* to me about it. Christ, this family is screwed up. No wonder I'm in therapy."

Penny smiled faintly. "You're right. But we are trying to fix it, Elsie." She extended her fingers toward Elsie, but Elsie stood up.

"Anyway, I didn't break the lamp."

"And neither did I." Penny hesitated. "Maybe the wind . . ."

"Yeah, right. In the middle of the night with the windows closed."

Penny looked reluctant. "Well, maybe . . . I hate to think a raccoon or possum got in here, but in these old houses you never know."

"Great. Now I'll really sleep well tonight."

Penny stood up, smiling. "I'll have your father look into it. Men love to track down wild animals. Makes them feel indispensable."

Elsie looked at her mother, a small frown on her face. "Mom, do you ever . . ."

Penny knew instinctively that Elsie was on the verge of sharing something terribly important with her, and she almost held her breath, waiting for it.

"What?" she encouraged.

And she saw decision waver in her daughter's eyes. Elsie said carefully, "Don't you think this place is weird? Creepy, like?"

Penny did not quite know how to respond. "Old houses often are."

Penny knew there was more. She could see it. But then Elsie just shrugged, and turned away. She walked over to the dresser and picked up the stone frog head, and Penny took that as a dismissal.

"Good night, honey. Just wanted to stop by and talk a little." And she thought, *I wish I were a better mother. How could I have turned out to be such a bad mother?*

"Mom." Elise turned abruptly to look at her when she reached the door. "I don't want you and Dad to stay together because of me. Do you understand? I don't want that."

Penny's throat was suddenly so tight that she couldn't speak, so she just nodded, and left quickly.

From the Diary of Elsie Mason

I wish Mom just had a clue of how hard it is to be her daughter. She's only Miss Perfect, Miss Size Six, Miss Not-Good-Enough-to-Be-an-Ordinary-Doctor-Had-to-Be-a-Freaking-Surgeon . . . And the bad thing is, you can't hate her for it. Like Dad says, she is important. And she does try so hard.

Maybe I should have told her about the woman. Like that wouldn't give her something to talk to Dr. T. about. And you see how far I got when I tried to talk to the old man about it. Star Trek! Right. But the way he looked at me when he said,

"Do you hear voices?" Like he was just looking for an excuse to slap the manacles on and cart me away. You know what would be a nice invention? A parent you could trust.

She was in the garden this afternoon, that strange woman, right there by the stone bench, looking at that piece of frog statue . . . and then she wasn't. That makes what? Five, six times I've seen her? As clear as daylight, too. Just here one minute, and then not. What *is* this?

And I'll tell you what else was strange. It was like only a few minutes that I was out there watching her—maybe ten—and when I went back inside hours had passed! Tell me that's not strange.

And then there's the talking. God, I don't know how many times I've heard that. I mean, for the longest time I'd think someone had left the television on, and then I'd remember we don't even have a television. It's really just so weird, but also kind of exciting. I mean, in a way I wish there was someone to talk to about it, to help me figure it out. But in another way, it's kind of cool that I'm the only one who knows, like being a superhero or something, and when I do figure it out maybe it will change the world. Ha!

I think maybe I will call Aunt Cathy, though, and see what she can find out about this place. Maybe it's one of those—what do you call them? hot spots?—like the Bermuda Triangle or crop circles.

But I'll tell you one thing. I've decided this house isn't haunted after all. It's a time portal. And sometimes I wish it would just swallow me up.

It's times like these a girl really needs to talk to her best friend. I wish Jill weren't such a dork.

SEVEN

The dark-haired woman walked right past me without seeing me, so close I might have reached out my hand and grabbed her arm—but I was afraid to. I stood between the door and the dresser, and I actually shrank back to flatten myself against the wall as she moved toward me. She did not even glance in my direction.

Oh, how my heart pounded. How icy was my skin, how dry my lips. I tried to speak and could not make a sound. My head throbbed with words and images, bits and pieces of the drama I had just witnessed flashing in my mind's eye like heat lightning on a dark horizon. I did not know what to make of it. I didn't try to understand it, not then. I wanted to know only one thing. "My dear, are you all right?" I said at last, in a voice that was breathless and barely audible.

I said it because the girl, the child I was so certain was Sarah, had put down her pen and wiped a tear from her face with an impatient swipe. She looked so alone and forlorn, trying so hard to be grown-up and blasé, and I was flooded with tenderness for her. I moved toward her instinctively, and started to repeat the question, but I stopped in midmotion, everything within me stilled by a sudden undeniable truth.

Ghosts did not cry.

Nor did they lie on beds in twilight-dim rooms and have conversations about school and doctors and troubled marriages.

I whispered, "Sarah?"

But her head was bent again over her writing, and she did not reply. I had not the breath to try again, my heart was pounding so. I folded my hands across my waist as though with that gesture I might physically keep myself from flying apart, and that was when my eyes fell upon the dresser.

My frog. The decapitated head of my frog, scarred and dirty, which only moments ago I had liberated from its forgotten grave, which moments beyond that had rested in the hands of a stranger. I reached for it with an unsteady hand, but my hand closed upon nothing.

I staggered back and spun quickly around. She was gone. One moment lying upon the bed with pen and book, the next, gone. The room itself seemed to shimmer and alter subtly, but I barely paused to notice.

"Sarah!" I cried. I cast my eyes frantically about, then raced from the room.

I plunged down the stairs, into the darkened foyer, to the parlor, the kitchen, the back room. All was still, dim and deserted.

"Where are you?" I shouted, foolishly and futilely. "Answer me!"

But no one was there.

I sank back against a wall and closed my eyes, drawing breath in and out, in and out, concentrating on nothing but that. No one was here. The house was empty. They were gone.

And yet an odd sort of exhilaration mingled with the despair that filled me, because they *had* been here, the woman I did not know and sweet Sarah, they had been here—or *somewhere*—as clearly as I was now. I had seen them and heard them and been close enough to touch them, and what miracle this might be I couldn't begin to guess. But it was a miracle. Of that I was certain.

I walked slowly through the house, my thoughts racing. Snatches of their conversation, details of their faces, their subtle movements and the background sounds of clothing that rustled and bedsprings that creaked—real, undeniably real. And then . . . not.

The lamp. With a sudden electric tingling of my hands and face I remembered the lamp I had thrown against the wall in my frustration, a broken lamp *they* could not explain. I rushed into the parlor, searching for it, the little cobalt lamp that had sat so charmingly on a pie table before the window. But of course it was gone.

The frog. The lamp. There was a connection somehow.

It was like peering through a window on another world; yes, that was it exactly, a window that could close as abruptly and as unpredictably as it opened. I could see them but they could not, for whatever reason, see or hear me. And sometimes that window opened, allowing me into their world, and them into mine. Other times the window remained closed, and other times it disappeared altogether.

But what world was it, precisely, that I was looking into? Nothing in my experience or philosophy had prepared me for this; of that I was certain. I had no basis from which to begin to understand it. Yet it was undeniably true.

I came out onto the porch, and I caught my breath. He was there, standing with his hands braced upon the rail like a man preparing to go to war, his stance set, his gaze directed out over the front garden. Solid. Real. Six steps away from me, and in another world.

For the longest time my legs were frozen to the floor; I couldn't move; I couldn't breathe. I was afraid even to blink lest he disappear as the others had done. I wanted to drink in every detail, to store them in my memory like ammunition against encroaching doubt—the drape of his shirt, the rough fabric of his trousers, the wave of hair against the back of his collar, the shadow on his neck. The sound of insects and the whisper of a breeze. Real. Yes, real. So real I almost could touch him . . . but I did not dare.

Hesitantly, as though I were treading on glass, I moved closer, circling toward the edge of the porch so that I might see him more clearly. I spoke before I could stop myself. "Jeff? Please . . ."

He turned, and his face registered surprise. "Oh! I'm sorry, I didn't hear you come up."

My breath dried up in my lungs; my muscles stiffened into leather; I am certain my heart forgot to beat for several attenuated moments.

He recovered himself and gave an embarrassed smile. "Were you looking for someone?"

And when I just stood there, still-eyed, breathless, gaping at him, his smile faded into puzzlement and polite concern. "Are you lost?"

There was a sound inside, perhaps a voice or a rattle of a

pan or the squeak of a door, and we both turned toward it. It was only for the flash of a second, but when I looked back, he was gone.

This time I didn't call out, nor race wildly through the house looking for him. I knew I wouldn't find him, yet I knew he was not gone.

I pressed my fingers against my lips and I wept quietly for joy.

I SAID, "You told me they were dead."

"Who?"

"My husband and my daughter."

"I'm quite sure you're the one who said that. I merely agreed with you."

"Perhaps you're right."

Oh, how very calm my voice was, and how proud I was of that. A few days ago I would not have been calm. I would have come raging into Michael's presence, beating on him with my fists, shouting wild accusations, making irrational-sounding claims at full pitch and as quickly as I could form them. But the fevered storm of emotion had passed, and in the interim I had glimpsed my little family—those strange, beloved faces living their unfamiliar lives in the space we shared but could not breach—again and again.

One might think that such inexplicable and repeated visitations would cause me to increasingly doubt my sanity. On the contrary. For the first time, the only thing I was entirely certain of was my own reason.

"However," I added, looking the wise and unflappable Michael strong in the eye, "what if we were mistaken?"

He lifted an eyebrow, nothing more. I took that as an invitation to continue.

"What if they were simply dead to *me*? And knowing that my husband had moved on with his life, married another, that my child, who would have been too young to remember the accident, now called another woman Mother . . . what if, never expecting me to recover, knowing how very many years I had been ill and that I could never reclaim what I had lost, you thought it was a kindness to let me believe my family was gone? I could forgive you for that."

He smiled gently. "Thank you."

I continued to gaze at him steadily and thoughtfully. "But that's not what happened, is it?"

He did not reply. It was his way.

"What if," I said very slowly, very carefully, and never once wavering in my gaze, "there is not just one world, one life, one reality . . . but many? As many realities as there are possibilities? And what if in one of those worlds the accident that killed my family did not happen, and they continue to live— only of course they live a completely different life than the one I knew with them?"

" 'In my father's house there are many mansions,' " he murmured. He seemed interested. "I have heard of such theories."

There was a theory. I exulted inside. It was a possibility. "And what if . . ." Here I took a breath. "What if, because of something the accident did to me, or some reaction I had to the medications I must have been given during the time I don't remember, or . . . or simply because God is good, what if I were able to see into that world now and then, and hear the conversations they had with one another, and know that their lives went on?"

"Then," he said, watching me now as I had watched him, "I imagine that would be a great comfort to you."

I wanted to slap him. I actually had to clench my fists and

tense my leg muscles to keep from springing on him. Perhaps I was not quite so in control of my emotions as I had first believed.

And yet I had gained something in the way of confidence and competency since I had last seen him, and I knew that my refusal to be provoked was the only way I could prove it to him—and to myself. I rose to the occasion.

"It would," I agreed levelly, "if the images I saw of them were of happy family life. Or one might even argue that images of discord or imminent disaster were projections of my own anxious imagination. . . ."

A faint smile of gratification touched his lips, acknowledging how quickly I had caught on, and I in turn felt proud.

I continued, "But the scenes I see are both happy and sad. They are also occasionally meaningless and boring. Just like life. I have searched a great many books on neurological disorders—my husband's library is filled with them—and there is no disorder that could account for this kind of hallucination."

"Actually," he said, still smiling, "there are a great many. But I do not think any of them account for your experience."

I had not expected him to capitulate so easily, and I was emboldened by his candor. "Perhaps," I suggested, "that is because you know exactly what does account for my experience. And perhaps you know that because you caused it, you and your colleagues who claimed so earnestly to want only to help me."

He said, "Suppose you tell me in more detail what it is precisely you've seen."

I gazed at him steadily for a time, trying to pry the truth from behind his kind, unyielding features. "You are the keeper of a great many secrets, Michael. Isn't it time you shared some of them with me?"

"No," he said simply, "not yet."

Then, "Please tell me what it's been like for you. I do very much want to know."

I had not planned to do that. The encounters were so personal, so intimately and completely my own, that the mere thought of sharing them with another seemed to diminish them somehow. They were, in fact, when I considered it, the only memories I could completely call my own. But as I looked into his gentle, compelling eyes I found I had no choice, and that, in fact, sharing my experiences with him was the one thing, above all in the world, that I wanted to do. And as I began to relate the events, the snatches of conversation—my sweet Sarah, the woman I did not know, and finally Jeff who could see me, who had spoken to me—as I spoke of these things, and relived them out loud for another, they seemed to grow in power, to become even more real.

Michael listened with quiet, interested eyes, interrupting only to ask a salient question, and as I spoke my secret memories I could feel a new understanding begin to grow between us, an element of trust I had never really experienced before. When I finished, he was silent for a time.

Then he said, "I do envy you."

I was startled. "Me? You envy me? Why?"

"Oh, for so many reasons." For a moment his gaze was faraway, his expression soft with emotions I could not read. "To live without a past is to live completely in the moment, and in the moment, anything is possible."

I was disappointed, and my tone showed it. "So," I said, preparing to rise. "You think my story is the product of a demented imagination after all. I can't think why I had ever allowed myself to hope you might see things otherwise."

"But that is not the only reason I find myself envious of you," he continued as though I had never spoken. "Do you realize what an extraordinary woman you must be, to have this opportunity to glimpse another world, even to participate in it? Why do you imagine you should have been chosen for such a thing?"

Now I was confused. Wary, but confused. "What do you mean?"

"Surely you agree that such encounters as you described are not of the ordinary world."

Cautiously, I agreed, "I never proposed they were."

He looked at me for a time, as though expecting me to say more. I did not dare.

In a moment he said, "Haven't you given any thought at all as to what the meaning of all this might be?"

I had thought of very little else, and I had reached no conclusion whatsoever. "Must everything have a meaning? Perhaps there is no meaning in it all, merely a happening, a circumstance, odd but true, an accident of time and space upon which I, for no particular reason at all, happened to stumble."

"Everything," he said with absolute conviction, "has a meaning. And until we understand what that meaning is, nothing is real."

I did not puzzle over that for long. I had become accustomed to dismissing his bits of arcane philosophy with the same absent notice with which one might brush dust from one's sleeve or shake out crumbs from a napkin. I said, "It doesn't matter why. It doesn't even matter whether or not you believe me. What matters is that I find a way to talk to them."

"Why?"

"Jeff is the key. It makes sense, though, doesn't it? He was the one person I didn't forget; the one thing the accident couldn't wipe from my mind was our love . . . the kind of love that could survive across time, across worlds. He *saw* me, Michael!" I couldn't keep my voice from rising with the wonder; nor could I keep the excitement out of my face. "He spoke to me, I was real to him! If it happened once it can happen again, and if he can see me, he can hear me!"

"But he didn't recognize you," Michael pointed out. "Why do you think that was?"

I dismissed him. "It was dark; there was barely a moment. . . . The important thing is that there was *contact*. Don't you understand how remarkable that is?"

"Why is it so important to communicate with them?" he repeated.

"Because," I answered slowly, "I think things aren't going well for them in this new life. I think they need me."

"Just as you need them."

"They are my family. They are the ones I love more than anything in the world, and seeing them has brought all those sleeping memories of love to life again. Of course I need them. And I need desperately for them to be happy."

"So you will give them happiness. . . ."

"If I can."

"And they will give you . . . ?"

He left the question unfinished, and I hesitated, not because I did not know the answer but because the answer was almost to precious to speak.

"A second chance," I whispered at last.

Michael nodded, and was silent. My gratitude to him for that was so intense it was almost reverent.

I said again, "It doesn't matter whether you believe me or not."

He smiled. "I know that."

"But I wish that you did."

"Then I do."

"Somehow that seems less than sincere." But I was not annoyed with him, or even disappointed anymore. He was kind, and he genuinely meant the best for me, and in his own way, I think he did believe me.

I smiled at him. "You are better to me than I deserve, I think."

He said, "No one could be better to you than you deserve."

His tone was so quiet, and his gaze so compelling, that I dropped my eyes for a moment, a little flustered. He let the seconds tick by, the tangle of emotions tie themselves into knots, before he spoke again.

And then he said, "What do you think happens after death?"

I felt something slam shut inside me. The tender moment evaporated like fog in the sun.

"It doesn't matter," I said shortly, "because they're not dead." I stood up. "I must get back. I've been gone too long already."

To my surprise, he let it drop. "I've enjoyed our time together."

I looked at him. "I believe in life after death," I said, "and resurrection in Christ our Lord." Odd, how easily those words came to me. But I couldn't remember where I'd learned them. "I believe," I added firmly, "that the spirit survives, and we go on living. What do you think happens? After we die, I mean."

He merely smiled. "Oh, I don't believe in death."

He came over to me and touched my arm lightly. The warmth penetrated me like a friendly embrace. "Good-bye, Mary. I hope you find what you need in these encounters. Please come to see me again soon."

I searched his face. "I need to know that this is real."

"You already know that."

"No, I . . ." Now I was flustered again, and confused. I took a breath, deep and long. I looked him square in the eye. "You're right. This has nothing to do with you. I thank you for your help, but . . . I must deal with this alone."

A fleeting sadness crossed his face. "You're wrong," he said. "It has everything to do with me, and I'm afraid I haven't helped you at all. Despite that, I hope you will come to see me again."

He looked so earnest, so sincerely in doubt of himself, that I had to smile. "I'll always come back to you, Michael," I said. "You make me angry sometimes, and you have no right to keep from me the things that you know and I do not . . . but I think, in your own way, you mean the best for me. And you didn't laugh at me and my strange tale. So I'll come back."

He seemed reluctant to let me go, and at the same time hesitant to speak. I wanted to leave, and quickly, before he said what I knew he must inevitably say. But something in his eyes held me there, waiting, until he said, "Mary . . . guard your heart. Things are not always what they seem."

And I replied, hating the necessity for it and hating the honesty that forced me to do so, "I know." Hard words. I almost choked on them. But to show him I was unafraid, and to convince myself, I took a breath, met his gaze, strengthened my voice, and repeated, "I know."

DISCOVERY

~

EIGHT

I began to uncover the truth on the day I learned to work the stove. It was such a simple thing, really, so obvious, I cannot understand how it could have eluded me for so long. One turned a knob, and the surface glowed hot. How clever. How easy. It occurred to me that there was no reason in the world why the more complex pieces of my missing memory should not fall into place in an equally simple way.

And so I fried bacon and made apple pancakes with a jar of applesauce I found in the pantry, and I ate with a deep and delightful appetite that seemed to me the first in many long ages. The sun had just cleared the misty row of trees outside the yellow-curtained window when I was finished, and the kitchen was bathed with a soft pink light as I tidied up. I spent some moments gazing thoughtfully at that window, remembering the cozy family scene I had observed from the other side of it, and how it had all disappeared when I raced inside. It would have been here, at this very table where they sat. It would have been there, on the stone path that curved eastward, where I stood. They might not have observed me, watching them, in the dusk. But there was no way I could have mistaken them.

And then there was Jeff, of course, on the porch. *He* had seen me. He had spoken to me. And he would do so again; of that I had no doubt. All I had to do was find him.

The most frustrating thing about these encounters was their apparent randomness, and try as I might I could think of no single factor that they all had in common, nothing I had done or had not done that might have triggered them. They did not occur at regular intervals nor in a single place. It was like a door swinging erratically in the wind, and when that door slammed shut there was nothing I could do to open it again.

Somehow I had to find the key. With the key I could find Jeff. And once we were together again, all would be right; everything would make sense. Today I had unlocked the mysteries of the stove; the mysteries of the universe could not be far behind.

And with such heady confidence to bolster me, I was not at all surprised to return to my upstairs bedroom and find it was occupied. But it was not Jeff who waited for me there, but Sarah.

She didn't see me at first. I was very still, hovering in the doorway with barely a breath, drinking in the sight of her and the world in which she lived with such wonder, such grateful astonishment, that the entire inside of me was filled with it and I hardly had room to think, much less breathe.

She sat at a desk in front of the window, wearing a short, soft cotton shirt that exposed her plump thighs. Her legs were tucked back on the rungs of her chair, and her hair was tousled in spikes and curls, shadowing her cheeks and her eyebrows. The window was open and the white curtains stirred. On the upper panes a thin mist had congealed, left over from the night. I could smell the breeze, gentle and morning-cool, slightly wet like the deep woods. She wrote in a journal with a lavender flowered cover, and her handwriting was tiny and precise.

Sometimes, if I listen hard enough, I can hear the clank, clank, clank from the boathouse, like something trying to break in, and I want to go there and stand on the ledge and look deep into the black water and see myself there, cold and floating at the bottom. I think about it a lot, just getting up in the middle of the night and walking barefoot across the grass and unlocking the boathouse door with the key from the hook in the kitchen, and going in and just looking. . . . I don't know for what. I wouldn't turn on the light, but maybe there would be a moon, and maybe in that little triangle of water where the boat doesn't quite meet the dock there would be something to see, and when I think about what it might be my heart pounds and my hands get clammy. Like with excitement maybe. But more like fear. Our cove is the deepest in the lake, Dad says. Almost seventy-five feet. You can't help but wonder what's down there, way, way down in the black water. You can't help wanting to find out.

What odd sad words for a young girl to write, and I wanted to touch her hand, to stop her pen. But all I could do was look at her, and want . . . so much.

I watched her until I thought my heart would break from watching her, and then an awful fear began to tighten inside me, the dread that if I stood in silence much longer she would disappear as she had on so many occasions before and I would have missed my chance; there still would be nothing but silence to mark the occasion. So I whispered urgently, "Sarah!"

She did not look up. I moved into the room.

I said again, "Sarah." Though I managed to put more strength into my voice, it still quavered a bit, in time with the knocking, pulsing jerking of my nerves. "Sarah, please."

She did not appear to hear me.

I wanted to touch her. How I longed to rush to her and drop to my knees and fold her in my embrace, or even to step quickly beside her and smooth away the curls from her forehead, to feel the springy dark silkiness of her hair and her dewy skin against my fingers. But I dared not try to penetrate the delicate fabric of time and space that separated us. I dared not risk losing her again.

I moved close, as close as I dared, until I was standing next to the window, within arm's reach of the desk where she sat. So close that my shadow would have fallen across her page had the sun shone with equal brilliance in both our worlds, so close that I could almost hear her breathing.

Her pen stopped moving upon the page. Her shoulders seemed to stiffen, and she raised her head slowly, her eyes fixed upon the window. I held my breath as she swiveled her head toward me by inches and fractions of inches, moving with the care one takes when trying not to startle a bird, or is fearful that what one has spied from the corner of one's eye might take a different shape when viewed full on, slowly, slowly, until she was looking directly at me.

Her eyes were wide and dark and her lips slightly parted for breath. She whispered, "Who are you?"

Oh, how my heart leapt and sang! Oh, how I wanted to rush to her and sweep her up and dance with her and cry, *I am here, I am here, I've found you and I've come home!*

I pressed my hands to my face to restrain my eagerness, my joy, my tears, the voice that wanted to cry out with sobs of joy, and desperate ticking seconds passed before I could reply simply, "Sarah? Is that you?"

She stood slowly, the little desk chair scraping over the corner of the braided rug and making a rattling sound against the pine floor. She said again, "Who are you?"

I said, "I've been ill. I know I've been away for a long time, but I'm home now. Please, darling, don't be angry. . . ."

She frowned at me, and I began to see that what I had taken for anger or mistrust was actually an expression of intense concentration and puzzlement. She said, "Are you real? Are you really here? You look real. Do something, move or something, if you're real." She cleared her throat, and seemed to be trying to gather a measure of authority about her, and she said, in a slightly louder tone, "Come closer if you're real."

Obligingly, I moved toward her a few steps. But as I did so she gasped and stumbled backward. She knocked over a desk lamp and fumbled to right it, in the process spilling a bottle of fragranced lotion. She said under her breath, staring at me, "Holy shit!"

I frowned sharply. "Where did you learn to use language like that?"

The bottle of lotion leaked a pink-scented puddle onto the desk, but she did not notice. She said, big-eyed, "Jesus, what are you? *Who* are you?"

I cast about for some sensible answer to that, and found none. I found instead only more questions. "Please tell me how you came to be in this place, and how I can get to you, or bring you to me. Listen to me, darling, we may not have much time. . . ."

She said, "I've seen you before, lots of times. But when I see you, it's like you're in a different dimension, a different place . . . like the scenery around you is all weird and changed, or sometimes you're in a room that's *like* the one I'm in only it's not. . . ."

She was talking fast now, and breathing fast, her words stumbling over each other in excitement. And though I was fascinated by what she said, my own questions and concerns were bubbling up inside and it was difficult not to interrupt her.

"You've never been this close before," she went on, eyes flickering over me, up and down, bright with wonder and hesitant belief. "Close enough to touch, only . . ." She extended a hesitant hand toward me, and withdrew it quickly, as though afraid of being burned, before I could even reach out my own. "The other day in the garden you were close, but not like this—"

"Yes!" I exclaimed, unable to restrain myself a moment longer. "Yes, the frog is mine, the one you found—the one we both found." I went quickly to it, started to pick it up, and then remembered how my hand had gone through it the last time I tried. My hand had gone through it—and abruptly the world in which she lived was gone. I dared not risk it.

But I looked at the stone frog, still dusted with the remnants of its grave and now endangered by a creeping puddle of creamy pink, and I said, "I saw you there, too. I followed you, and . . ."

But my words trailed off as I remembered the confusing

and less-than-happy ending to that evening. The woman who had been here, the conversation they had, the puzzles I did not want to think about.

She was staring at the frog. "The statue? The frog?" She looked at me. "That was what you were looking for!"

I nodded impatiently. "Yes, I told you, it's mine. And now you have it. You found it and brought it here. . . ."

Again my words trailed off because I could not think of how that could be; there was no explanation I could offer that made sense and no further comment on the subject to make. And she was gazing at me in a most peculiar way.

"Oh, my God," she said softly. "You said something. What? What are you trying to say?"

An awful suspicion began to creep over me. "Sarah? Can you hear me?"

"You're trying to tell me something!" she said on a breath. "What is it?"

A desperate despair filled me. "Look at me!" I pleaded. "Try to understand me. I have so much to ask you. Darling, this is so important! How can I reach you if I can't talk to you!"

Again her eyes were big with wonder. "Oh, my God. I can see you talking, but I can't hear anything you're saying. Can you hear me?"

"Yes!" I cried. And then, remembering she couldn't hear me, I nodded my head vigorously.

She whispered, "Holy shit." And again, "Holy shit. I'm not believing this."

I was too desperate by now to reprimand her for her language. "Sarah, you must believe me. Don't turn away from me, please. . . ."

I reached out to her, but her eyes had begun to roam the

room, searching for something. Her gaze fell upon the desk and she lurched for it.

She snatched up her journal and tore a page from it. She held it and a pen out to me urgently. "Okay, maybe this is crazy, but . . . you know I've heard about automatic writing, and maybe it's something like this . . . maybe you could write down what you want to say. Can you write it down?"

I said, "I don't think—"

But with the impatience of youth she did not wait for me to finish. She turned quickly to the desk and wrote something on the paper in quick, excited strokes. She held the paper up for me to read.

Elsie Marie Mason, she had written.

"That's my name," she said. "Can you write yours? Can you tell me where you are and what it's like there and . . . and how did you get here? How do you keep disappearing? Who are you? What do you want to tell me?"

At last she took a breath, seeming to realize the over-whelming nature of her questions. She laid the paper carefully on the desk, and the pen next to it. "Please," she said, her eyes begging. "Write your name."

I stared at the paper. Elsie Marie Mason. Not Sarah. Elsie Marie. My head reeled with confusion and uncertainty, and I thought, *No. It's a mistake—it has to be. Your name is Sarah; it must be Sarah. . . .*

So many questions, too many, and none of them with an-swers I wanted to hear. Elsie Marie Mason.

I moved to the window and lifted my finger to the misty pane. Already the warming sun had begun to melt the fog on the glass, cutting waving rivulets through its opacity. I heard Sarah—no, Elsie Marie—gasp as my fingertip formed another

line, and joined it with another. M-A-R-Y. One by one I
carved the letters into the mist.

"Mary," I said. "My name is Mary."

But when I turned, she was gone.

THE MORNING WAS MISTY, and when she stepped out into
the garden she could feel the cool fingers of it caress her cheek
and play with the folds of her skirt. She drew her shawl up over
her head to protect her hair, which always curled too wildly on
mornings like these, and she went down the cobbled path with
a basket of bread over her arm, feeling like a character in a fairy
tale. The bread was for Jenny Fowler, who lived around the
corner and who was down with a broken ankle. It smelled of
cinnamon and yeast, and she had been up since four A.M. baking it. Not that she minded. She liked the quiet before the
family was awake, a good time to collect her thoughts and plan
her day, to get the old stove started and the kitchen nice and
warm before the baby woke.

Smoky delphiniums nodded their heads with the weight of
the dew, and even the brilliant zinnias were muted, yellows,
oranges, reds all overcast with a hue of gray. The sky was solid
silver, blotting out the distant mountains, but she knew that
in only a moment the clouds would part and the faded purple–
shadowed ranges would come into view, flower gardens and
picket fences would pop into color, children's voices would fill
the yards, dogs would bark, laundry would wave in the breeze.

Across the narrow street and separated by an expanse of
pretty yard, she could see the yellow light from the windows
of the Mitchells' small white house, and farther down the road
a screen door bounced closed. Myra Hamlin, out to collect
her paper and put down a pie plate of food for the ten stray

cats she claimed were not her own. She could see the church steeple from here, and a portion of the iron-fenced churchyard, and across the street a white building with LIVERY stenciled on the front, although no horses had been kept there in anyone's memory. Next door was the brick post office, and as she watched a light came on in the window. Netty Baker opening for business; that would make it seven o'clock on the dot.

She stood there smiling for a breath or two, looking around this gentle, lovely place, letting herself be filled with that sweet, soft contentment that came so rarely but almost always in quiet moments like these. As she moved to unlatch the gate she heard a sound behind her, and glanced over her shoulder to see the door to her husband's office open. He came out, pulling on a jacket, and he lifted his hand to her to wait.

She felt her heart swell as he approached, this man she loved, so handsome and so strong, and still, after all this time, capable of speeding her pulse with a glance, and she thought that it was true, what she had heard, that happiness was not in the great things but the small; happiness was moments like this. He smiled a tender greeting as he dropped his hand onto her shoulder, and as they walked through the gate together she was thinking, *Don't let me wake up, don't let me . . .*

Penny awoke bathed in the glow of the dream that was so clear she could still feel the remnants of the dew in her hair and on her skin. She lay there with her eyes closed, smiling, trying to drift back into that time and place, until another, even more pleasant sensation beckoned her to wakefulness. Bacon. The smell of frying bacon on a damp lake morning. Sunday. It was Sunday, a time for sleeping late and making pancakes and reading the paper in the hammock on the porch. Sunday. She hadn't slept so well in a year.

The morning was silvery gray, just like in her dream. She paused a moment at the window, looking out over the lake, lingering in the contentment, the quiet joy of early mornings and glowing windows and fresh-baked bread. She loved mornings like this: quiet, misty. Warm with the presence of family and the smell of breakfast.

She smiled at the sentiment, both because it was so unlike her and because, these days at least, it was unlikely. But today felt different. She went downstairs in her nightshirt and for the first time that summer she forgot to be afraid of the kitchen.

"You made—" she began cheerfully as she entered the kitchen, then stopped and looked around. Paul was at the breakfast table in his damp T-shirt and jogging shorts, munching on a Danish and sipping a paper cup of coffee as he read the paper. "Bacon," she finished lamely.

It was Sunday. He always jogged to the minimart for the paper and she never ate breakfast. He hadn't even made coffee.

He looked up. "What?"

"Nothing." She went over to the island, filled the pot with water, measured out the coffee. "I just thought it would be a good day for pancakes and bacon."

"Great idea." He started to get up. "Is there bacon in the fridge?"

"Not unless you bought it."

He sat down again. "Sorry about the coffee. I would have made a pot, but didn't think you would be up this early."

"That's okay." She shrugged easily and went over to the cabinet, opening it. "It's nice out this morning, isn't it? It reminds me of when we first got this place, and we used to sit out on the porch and watch the fog on the lake and make up Indian ghost stories, remember?"

He made a soft appreciative sound. "God, it's been forever since I thought of that. Those were good days."

"We've had lots of good days here." She smiled, and the way he looked at her made her realize how long it had been since he had seen her smile.

He said, "I like to hear you talk like that. What put you in such a good mood?"

She wanted suddenly to tell him about the dream, about the misty, pale garden colors and the yellow-lit windows and the church steeple, and how real it all had been, and the strange, quiet, good feeling it had left inside her. But when she opened her mouth to do so she suddenly got a mental glimpse of the face of the man from her dream, and it wasn't Paul's.

She said, "Oh, nothing. Just a good night's sleep, I guess."

She turned quickly back to the cabinet. "Have you seen the applesauce?"

NINE

The trouble with knowing what your dog really thinks about you, the boy decided, is that afterward it's very hard to be bad.

—*THE BOY WHO COULD SPEAK DOG,* PAUL MASON

The Boy Who Could Speak Dog was a story Paul used to tell Elsie when she was small and her mother worked twelve to twenty-four hours a day. He actually started making up the tale when she was an infant and the sound of his voice seemed to soothe her colic, or help her fall asleep after a bout of fretfulness. By the time she was three or four she would beg for installments, and he would make up a new outrageous adventure for boy and dog every night while she cuddled in his arms in her footed pajamas, or bounced with excitement on her Peter Rabbit sheets.

One day, on a whim, he decided to write the story down, perhaps submit it to a children's magazine, or at the very least have it bound to give to Elsie for her birthday when she was old enough to appreciate it but not so old as to be embarrassed by it. To his surprise the little story began to grow, to take on a more sophisticated undertone than he had intended, to actually have merit.

When he was finished he knew he had a nice piece of work, perhaps even publishable, although he did not know enough about the children's market to even raise a hope. He never expected it to be hailed as an instant classic, or to have his name mentioned in one breath with Antoine de Saint-Exupery, or to have the little tome sell over a million copies in its first year.

The first five years of snowball success were fantastic. After years of penury on a high school teacher's salary, and more than a little anxiety about the mounting eduational loans both he and Penny had accumulated, money was suddenly not a concern. The fame embarrassed him at first—it was just a children's book, after all—but when his picture started appearing in *Publisher's Weekly* in conjunction with articles about the foundation upon which publishing houses were built, and when he actually had to hire a secretary to handle all the requests for speaking engagements, he began to appreciate it.

His next book performed only moderately well, the book after that even less impressively. No one seemed to notice. The sales from *The Boy Who Could Speak Dog* remained steady; there was an animated feature, and talk of a Saturday-morning cartoon show.

Meantime, Penny finished her residency and joined a prestigious surgical practice near Duke University. Paul was offered a professorship at the Woodlands, which he accepted, not because of the money, which was outrageous for the position, nor because of the fact that he was required to deliver only two lectures a month, nor even because of the almost implicit promise of tenure—but because of the prestige.

By then he hadn't written a word in over six years and the sheen on *The Boy Who Could Speak Dog* was growing a little dull. At faculty parties he talked a lot about his new work and the depth of research it required, and how difficult it was in the publishing world to move beyond a genre, but at home he mostly jotted down ideas. Not that it mattered. He was Paul Mason, and his book was a classic.

When she was ten, Elsie was sent home from school with a headache, and by that night she was hospitalized with a temperature of one hundred and five. For forty-eight helpless, terrified hours he and Penny lived under the shadow of meningitis, paralysis, brain damage, death. And for forty-eight hours Paul sat uselessly in a hospital waiting room while Penny consulted with specialists, assembled a team, donned sterile garb to visit their daughter, talked in quick, clipped tones using words he didn't understand. When the phone rang, it was for her. When the nurse appeared, she asked for her. When questions were asked, she had the answers.

Paul did not realize what was happening at the time, because all of his mind, all of his attention, all of his world was focused on his little girl, for whom he could do nothing. But when he looked back he knew exactly when Paul Mason, author, began to disappear, melting into nothingness like salt in the rain.

It turned out Elsie did not have meningitis after all, merely a nasty reaction to an insect bite. But everything changed after that. He saw his wife differently. He saw himself differently.

One night she came home close to midnight, having been delayed by a page from the emergency room. She was wearing the wool skirt she had started out in, but her blouse had been replaced by a green scrub smock. When she was called to the emergency room it was usually because of a traffic accident, which meant massive bleeding, which meant stained and often ruined street clothes.

lways wanted to decompress when she came in late, ...ne talked about her surgery, which had gone well, and the hospital meeting, which had not, over a glass of wine. He listened, as he always did.

And then he said, "I never expected it to be like this."

She looked blank. "Like what? Do you mean because I'm late? You know that's part of the job, hon; it always has been. God knows it's not the first time."

"No. Like this. You. Me." He gestured with his glass, a small movement less uncertain than restrained. "I mean, I always knew you were going to be something. We both always knew that, didn't we? But I never expected to be . . . nothing."

She stared at him for the longest time, as though she was genuinely trying to make sense of what he'd said. Then she said, "Oh, for Christ's sake, Paul." She downed the last swallow of her wine and went to bed.

Four years later, when he was threatened once again with losing Elsie, when he was lost and angry and helpless and going through the motions of doing the right things and saying the right things and trying to be the perfect parent while Penny was in fact the perfect parent, the rock of decision and expertise and busyness, he asked a young student out for coffee. He knew how it would end, of course, though he pretended not to. He knew the girl had a crush on him. He knew she wanted to talk about more than eighteenth-century poetry, and he knew he was falling victim to the oldest cliché since higher education had begun. And he knew, in the end, he would be pitied by his colleagues not for his actions, or his lapse in judgment, nor his stupidity, but in fact for his utter lack of originality.

He talked too much and too honestly, not about her but about himself, about everything, for after all, who did he have

to talk to? Who could he say these things to? Penny had someone, Elsie had someone, but who did he have?

By the third night coffee had turned to wine, and on the
fourth night she said, "It's really strange when you think about
it. Without your daughter, there would have been no book.
And without the book, there would have been no you."

And that night he kissed her.

"A HELL OF A REASON to wreck a marriage," he muttered
out loud now. "Because you found someone to feel sorry for
you."

"I actually can't think of any good reason to wreck a marriage," said a voice behind him.

He was in his office, computer screen aglow and blank on
the desk before him, leaning back in his leather chair, gazing
out at the lake. Elsie had gone with her mother to town, and
the house was still and empty. He often talked aloud to himself, working out plot lines for novels that never quite made it
past the first chapter, or repeating a bit of dialogue he thought
might inspire something more. In the months of his separation
from Penny, after he had lost his job, he spent so much time
alone that his own was often the only voice he heard for days at
a time.

Still, he was startled and embarrassed to be caught talking
aloud, and when he spun around and leapt up from the chair,
he almost tripped.

"Excuse me?" he said, trying not to be annoyed. "Do I
know you?"

She said, "I'm not sure."

"Did my wife—" And then he remembered Penny wasn't
home and he changed the question to, "Who let you in?"

She was not, in actual fact, *in*. She stood on the threshold of the French door that opened onto the wraparound porch, framed by a glow of afternoon light, and she seemed relatively unconcerned about whatever invasion of privacy she might have committed. Rather, she gazed around the room with intense interest, studying everything—including himself—as though she intended to memorize it.

She said, "This is my house. My name is Mary."

"Oh." He relaxed a little as things began to make sense. "Are you related to the Greenfields? That's who we bought it from. Of course, it had been empty a long time by then."

"Everything looks . . . different."

"We've made quite a few changes." He looked at her more carefully. "You were here a couple of weeks ago, on the porch."

She looked surprised. "Was it that long?"

He debated only another second. "Would you like to come in? My wife isn't home, but I could show you around. We've really loved the place."

There was an odd, almost sad smile on her face when she looked at him. "That's the second time you've mentioned your wife. The third if you count your opening remark."

He didn't know how to respond to that. She came inside the room, leaving the halo of sun behind her, and as she did something seemed to change. It was almost as though the molecules within the room rearranged themselves subtly, thickening the air, sharpening the focus of angles and shadows, shivering a little, in the tiniest, almost imperceptible way, against the gentle force of her movement. Paul could feel the nerve endings on his arms and his legs tingle as though in response to an unseen electrical charge, and his mouth grew dry. He took an involuntary step backward, and then felt foolish for doing so.

He said, looking at her closely, "Do I know you?"

But she was looking out the window behind him, her eyes wide. "Was there a flood?"

"What?"

She gestured to the window, and he followed her gaze to the view beyond.

"Do you mean the lake?"

She took a few steps toward the window. "When did they build a lake?"

"In 1932."

She turned to him, moving as gently as a zephyr, and a small frown puckered her brow. "I don't remember that."

His laugh sounded forced and uneasy, and seemed to echo a little, as though the room were hollow. "I don't exactly remember it either."

She came over to the desk, passing close to him, and once again he had to stop himself from shrinking back. Only later would he realize what was so strange about her nearness, what made him so uneasy: she had no smell. No drift of perfume or hint of shampoo or embedded fabric softener in her clothing . . . no warm-flesh smell or sun-baked smell or lake-water smell, no sunscreen or hand-lotion or breath-mint smell; no smell at all. It was odd.

She was looking at the photographs on his desk, not touching them, just looking. His wedding picture. The picture of Penny holding a newborn Elsie in the hospital bed, all shiny-faced and beaming. A studio portrait of the three of them in an oval frame.

She said softly, "I don't know these people."

"That's my wife, and my daughter." He added, studying her profile, "Have we met before this? You look familiar to me."

She turned, her face suddenly alight. "Do I?"

"I just can't think where I might have met you before."

And the excitement in her face faded, even as she searched his eyes. "So you don't know me? You don't remember me at all?"

"Maybe if you told me your last name."

She said, still searching, still hoping for he knew not what, "Your name . . . it isn't Jeff, is it?"

"It's Paul. Paul Mason."

She lowered her lashes on a disappointment so intense he felt compelled to apologize for it.

"I'm sorry, but I'm confused. Were you expecting to meet someone else here? Could you have the wrong house?"

"No." A sigh, barely a breath. "I just . . . you look like someone I . . . I was hoping you would be . . . someone else." A quick desperation darted into her eyes as she looked up at him again. "You don't know Jeff? He was a doctor, and he used to live here, and a little girl called Sarah . . . Do you know what became of them?"

But before he could answer, even as he began to shake his head, she pressed her hands to her face with a sharp breath that sounded more like frustration than despair. "I don't understand! If you're not Jeff, who are you? What are you doing here, and why are you the only one who can hear me?"

"I told you, my name is Paul—"

"You don't know, do you?" Her gaze now was intent and focused, and laced with a little pity.

"Know what?"

She gave a little smile and turned one palm upward, gesturing around the room. "That you're not real. That none of this is."

Paul let a couple of breaths pass, watching her. "Can I call someone for you? Or drive you home?"

"No. There's nothing you can do for me." She moved away from the desk, toward the door. Her back was to him, and her shoulders seemed slumped, her gait tired. "I thought there was, but . . . I guess not."

He said, "If you'll just tell me where you live . . ."

She turned back to him suddenly, angrily. "I told you, I live *here*! Or somewhere *like* here. You're the one who doesn't belong, you and your wife and your little girl, and your pictures that aren't mine. You're not Jeff! Why are you talking to me?"

He spread his hands palms up, soothingly. "Lady, look, I don't know what your problem is, but—"

She drew a sharp breath, and the anger seemed to drain from her, leaving only the tired disappointment. "I don't know what the problem is either. Maybe you should ask your little girl. She seems to be better able to deal with this than either one of us."

Paul felt a needle stab of fear, irrational and probably completely unnecessary, go through him. "Elsie? You've spoken to Elsie?"

Her smile seemed bitter. "Not exactly."

"What did you say to her? When did you see her?"

She looked at him, searchingly, for what seemed to be a long time. And then her eyes clouded, seeming almost to fade from a brilliant green to a sad, dull hazel, and the fog that shrouded them was disappointment.

Paul felt an odd little prickle of guilt, because she had looked at him and had not found what she wanted.

"Don't wreck your marriage, Paul Mason," she said at last, and it was as though the sorrow of the world weighted her words. "Please don't do that."

He made a decision. "Listen, I don't want any trouble, but

I think you'd better leave now and not come back. I don't want to have to call the police." As he spoke, to give authority to his words, he turned to the desk to pick up the cordless phone. And when he turned back, she was gone.

Paul walked over and closed the French doors, hating himself for it, and, after a moment, he locked them.

TEN

They slept close together, boy and dog, until the morning light. The sound of the dog's steady breathing seemed as old as time, and it seemed to say, "You are safe with me."

—*THE BOY WHO COULD SPEAK DOG*, PAUL MASON

FROM THE DIARY OF ELSIE MASON

Whoever would have thought the old man would turn out to be useful—you might even say pivotal—*in something like this? In anything, really! But something this huge, that he would be the one. Unbelievable. But I guess I should start from the beginning, if I can even remember where the beginning is, since I wrote last. I look at that stupid stuff about the boathouse and it seems like years ago, like someone else wrote it, and who cares anyway? Let me tell you the only thing— the only thing!!—that anybody has written in this room that means anything at all—that's important at all!—are those four letters on the window. M-A-R-Y. All dripping and melting in the fog just like a gothic movie. Mary. And then what should he do at supper tonight just as casual as you please but start talking about this strange person who came by while we were gone saying she used to live here, and how he thought she was a little on the crazy side, and that her name was Mary!! Well, of course it couldn't be the same person, I didn't even think that, but then he looked straight at me with that concerned-daddy look and he said, "She said she knew you, hon. She said she'd talked to you." And I about wet my pants! I mean, holy shit, could it be? And he's saying, "Because I really don't like the idea of you hanging out with someone like that." And then Mom chimes in, "What do you mean, crazy? Isn't that something of a generalization?" And he says, "Well, if you'd only been here you could have made a diagnosis." And they go on like that for a while, you know how they do, and I'm thinking . . . well, I don't know what I'm thinking! Could it be possible? How could it be possible? But wouldn't it be something if my very own dad—I mean if he could actually see what I see?? What if I could talk to him, what if I could tell him, what if he could see her too? Well, he'd probably never believe me, think I was making it all up to get attention or something, but I know what I saw, and what I heard, and when he said that she said she used to live here, it gave me an idea. I mean, OK, it's like, hardly even possible that his Mary could be my Mary—I mean, how could a thing like that happen, anyway? The man has absolutely no imagination!—but when he said she used to live here, that was the idea!*

You know how I hate going to town and those damn "counseling" sessions, but Jesus, if I could make Thursday come faster! And why do we have to live way out in the middle of the goddamn sticks, anyway, where there isn't even a library!

Hey, I just thought of something. Maybe I should tell them Mary is someone I met in therapy. Ha!

"You keep looking at your watch," Dr. Turner said. He smiled. "Another appointment?"

"Actually, I do have something I'd rather be doing."

"I'm not going to force you to stay. If you'd rather catch up another time . . ."

"Yeah, like my mom would let me get away with that."

"This is about you, not your mom."

Elsie said impatiently, "No, really, let's just do it. I've got another half hour before Mom picks me up."

"So what is it you'd rather be doing?"

"Almost anything."

He waited patiently, in that way he had that seemed to wriggle confessions out of a person whether they wanted to make them or not, until Elsie said, "Aunt Cathy has some stuff for me. I'm just anxious to see it, that's all."

"Oh? What kind of stuff?"

"Just a photocopy of some pages from a book, about people who used to live around the lake."

"That sounds interesting. Does your dad have you on a project for summer vacation?"

"No. This is my own project."

"I didn't know you were interested in history."

"Just this history."

"Any particular reason?"

"My aunt Cathy says we had some ancestors who used to live there, back before there was a lake. I'd just like to know who they were, that's all."

"I understand your uncle Andrew is not doing all that well."

"He's got cancer. Mom says he's going to die."

"I'm sorry. Do you want to talk about it?"

"He's old. Everyone dies."

"It always seems much worse when someone dies young."

"I suppose. Aunt Cathy says there used to be a whole community there, before they built the lake. I mean, more of a community than there is now. That's why it has so much historical interest, and why somebody went to the trouble of writing down all the people who used to live there."

"Now, that *is* interesting. An old house, a lost ancestor, a town that used to be and is no more . . . sounds like something good to read on a rainy day."

She smiled a little. "All it needs is a ghost."

"If you need a term paper for school next quarter, you've already got a topic. I'd leave out the ghost, though."

"My old man doesn't call them term papers. He calls them 'expository writings.' "

"Maybe your dad won't be teaching you next year."

"Not that again." She wriggled impatiently in the chair, glanced at her watch. "I already told Mom I'm not going to that east Podunk boarding school she's so hot on. I'm not going anywhere. I like things the way they are."

"I can understand that. It would be hard starting school in a strange place, without your best friend."

She shrugged. "If you mean Jill, I can do without her."

"Oh? I thought you said you two had been best friends since first grade."

"Yeah, well, things change. People change." Again she shifted her weight uncomfortably, and looked at her watch. "Has this thing stopped or is this the longest hour on record?"

"How did Jill change?"

"You know." She shrugged. "Just changed. Got weird."

"Weird how?"

"What is this, the inquisition? I'm not going to rat out my friends, and what do you care anyway?"

"I care about everything that affects you. That's what I'm here for, to talk about your life, and what's important to you." He smiled. "That, as you so often point out, is what your parents pay me for." He waited a moment for this to sink in, and said, "Is that what you and Jill argued about? Her getting 'weird'?"

She hesitated. "I don't want anyone to get in trouble."

"You know that everything you tell me inside this room is confidential. We've talked about this before. There are only two ways I can break that confidence. The first is with your permission. The second is if I think that remaining silent would endanger you or someone else."

"You talk to my mom."

"I'm obligated to discuss your progress with her, but never the contents of our conversations. The most important thing in our relationship is that you trust me." He looked at her levelly. "Not that your mom agrees with me or that your dad likes me or even that I get paid. I've told you before, I'll do whatever I have to to earn your trust. So now I need to know: do you trust me or not?"

She was silent for a moment. Then, reluctantly, she answered, "Yeah. I guess."

"So what did you and Jill fight about? The drugs?"

She cast him a sly glance. "Yeah. Some. I mean, getting high now and then is one thing, but some of the stuff she does is just plain stupid. And then it makes her, well . . . stupid. Who wants to be around somebody like that? The stuff she talks about, the things she says. . . ."

"Like what?"

"Well . . . like dying and stuff. I mean, she's obsessed with it sometimes. Jesus. I mean, lighten up."

He waited. Silence was a trick of his. Sooner or later he knew she'd always fill it. She always said she wouldn't, and she always did.

"I mean, why does she have to be so crazy sometimes? It's not like she's serious or anything, but Jesus, the way things are today and the things kids do, it's just not cute anymore, is it?"

"What's not?"

"The way she talks."

"What way?"

"About, you know, stuff. I know it's just talk, but Christ, it creeps me out. Sometimes I think, I don't know, maybe I should, like, tell someone, you know? Like my mom or somebody, and she would tell Jill's mom, and that would put a stop to it, all right."

"Put a stop to what?"

"Everything. The craziness. Do you think I should tell?"

"What do you think?"

In a moment she shrugged. "I don't know. She just makes me so mad. What do I need that kind of trouble for? I'm not responsible for her. She should just grow up and get her act together."

"But you miss your best friend."

She was silent for a time, gazing at the opposite wall. "Yeah," she said, "sometimes. She's still a jerk, but if we move back to Chapel Hill, I might start hanging out with her again. I mean, maybe she *can't* get her act together by herself."

"People make choices, Elsie. In spite of everything we try to do to help, in the end, everyone is responsible for their own choices."

"I guess." She looked back at him. "But you know what

else I think? I think Jill is wrong. About dying, I mean. I think it's maybe *not* just being swallowed up by a big black pool. I think maybe you go on. I think maybe you go on and you have to make *up* for the things you did, or didn't do, while you were alive. Wouldn't that be a big fat joke on everyone, if you didn't get to die at all, but you had to *go on?*"

She hadn't realized how loud her voice had gotten until the silence fell, and the absence of her shrillness seemed to echo. She was breathing a little quickly, too, and it embarrassed her. She looked at her watch again, and got up. "My mom's probably here by now. I'll wait for her outside."

"I'M TELLING YOU, it was weird," Penny said. "And . . . really nice. I was in a whole other place, but it was home. It was home, but I've never been there. And the details! I knew the names of people, my neighbors—Myra Hamlin with all those cats, and Netty Baker the postmistress. There was a little white church with a steeple, and a livery across from it that wasn't used as a livery anymore, and a brick post office next to that. It was like being in a movie. And the garden. It was like my own garden, at the lake house, or like it would be if I had time to take care of it. It had the little picket fence and the ball-and-chain gate, and those flowers, the ones that come in all the colors, what are they called?"

"Zinnias?"

"No, taller than that—cosmos, that's it, and snapdragons and hollyhocks, a regular cottage garden like I've always wanted to have there. I was going to take bread to a neighbor who was sick—Jenny Fowler, that was her name—and can you just imagine that? Me, baking bread? And then the back door opened and my husband came out. Only it wasn't Paul."

"What happened then?" Cathy leaned her chin on her

folded hands, her latte forgotten on the table between her elbows.

"He came over to me, and smiled, and put his arm around me, and that was all. I guess we went on to see Jenny. But when I woke up, the feeling was . . . indescribable. As though I'd been on a long vacation, or as though I had just remembered the one thing in all the world that made me happy."

"Wow," Cathy said softly. "It's like you have a whole other life. You, Ms. Science-Is-Everything-and-the-Soul-Is-Made-Up-of-Chemicals-in-the-Brain, may have had a genuine out-of-body experience."

Penny frowned. "Don't be silly. It was just a dream, that's all. Better than the ones I usually have."

"You mean about the bloody kitchen?"

Penny repressed a shudder and picked up her coffee. "Please."

"You really should talk to Paul about the dreams. Both of them."

Penny was uncomfortable. "I know. But somehow . . . they just seem so personal. And I don't feel . . . I don't know. . . ." She groped for words. "Safe, I guess, sharing them."

"That's bad."

She sighed. "I know." She dropped her eyes to the cappuccino in front of her, absently stirring the melting froth with the tip of her spoon. "And sad. Used to be, Paul would be the first person I would want to run and tell about something like this. You know, he was so imaginative, so ready to jump into any scenario and play it out. . . ." She glanced up with a half grin. "Just like you, only more."

Cathy lifted an eyebrow. "I like that."

"He was such a kid." Her smile was a long time fading, and

she gazed wistfully into the past. "And the way he had of making you believe just about anything . . . I used to love the way he could do that." She came reluctantly back to the present and finished with a shrug. "We've both changed, I guess. But I do not believe the human soul is composed entirely of chemicals."

"He would have gotten a real kick out of this dream, though."

"The old Paul would have written a novel about it."

Cathy returned to her latte and sipped it thoughtfully for a moment. "You know what your dream reminds me of? The way you described the town, I mean?"

"What?"

"That painting by what's-his-name."

Penny laughed a little. "Norman Rockwell? Makes sense, doesn't it? Symbolizing my need to return to a simpler time."

"No, not Rockwell, that other fellow who does local landmarks. John Peters," she decided triumphantly. *"Mercy in 1920."*

Penny stared at her blankly for a moment, then exclaimed, "Mercy! That was the name of the community. It's on the post office, almost faded away. . . ." And her voice trailed off as she thought about the little redbrick post office, which might be visible from her front gate if not for the stand of poplar trees and the bank that had been formed by the bend in the gravel road. In her dream there had been no bank, but the road would have been rerouted, wouldn't it, when they built the lake?

She blinked and focused on Cathy again. "I didn't know there was a painting."

"Sure you did. It's on the cover of your phone book at the lake."

The phone book, of course. She must have looked at that

painting several times a week without seeing it. Penny felt an unaccountable sense of disappointment, even as she found that her lips were moving into a small, self-deprecating smile. "Ah, that explains it then. Some people try to escape their problems in drugs or alcohol. I escape mine in a phone book."

"Not necessarily," Cathy said.

"What?"

"I mean it doesn't necessarily explain it." When Penny just looked at her, Cathy added, "How did you know the names of the people?"

For a moment Penny had no answer; then she waved a dismissive hand. "From the phone book, I guess. It's not as though they were *real* people."

"What if they were?"

"God, Cat, you're as gullible as a six-year-old. You'll believe anything."

A shadow fell across Cathy's face. "Not anything."

Penny reached across the table and touched her fingers. "Don't mind me. I'm just jealous."

Cathy's eyes opened wide. "Of me?"

"Yes, of you. That you've managed to keep what I lost. I used to believe in anything, myself."

For a moment the two women smiled at each other, smiles that were filled with wistfulness and understanding. And then Cathy said, "That reminds me. I have that stuff for Elsie." She reached for her bag.

"Elsie?"

"You didn't know she called me?"

"She's not always very communicative," Penny answered, trying to keep the judgment out of her tone, "particularly with her parents."

Cathy just smiled. "What thirteen-year-old girl is?"

"What did she call you about?"

"I don't guess it's a secret." She pulled out a sheaf of papers from her purse. "She said you'd told her what I'd found out about the family—how we had ancestors who settled there after the Civil War, and that I was doing some research into the area—and she wanted to know if I knew how to find out everyone who'd lived in your lake house. As it happens, there's a book that lists all the property owners at the time the lake was built, and most of the listings have a paragraph or two on the genealogy of the house, if it's known. We only have one copy and I can't take it out of the library, but I photocopied that section for her. Of course, it will take a bit of ingenuity on her part to find out exactly which house is yours—they didn't exactly give addresses—but that should be the fun part for her."

"Well, what do you know?" Penny lifted an eyebrow. "I had no idea she was interested in history, and to hear her tell it she hates living at the lake." Her expression dropped wryly. "Of course, she hated living in town, too."

Cathy lowered her voice as though by doing so she might be forgiven the breaking of one of their unspoken luncheon rules. "Has there been any change?"

Penny just shook her head, dropping her eyes.

Cathy straightened her shoulders, and injected cheerfulness into her voice. "But this is a good sign, isn't it? That she's interested in this?"

"It will give her something to do besides sit in her room all day," Penny agreed.

"Oh, and that reminds me. It seems our family is just full of scandal. That ancestor of ours that I thought ended up settling out by the Lost Villages? He did establish a branch of the family out that way, and then *his* son or grandson got into some kind of scandal and was run out of town or changed his name or something—that's why it's taking so long to trace. But it's all kinds of exciting. I'm hoping to get some time with the microfiche reader this week—this kind of thing is so obscure it hasn't even made it to the computer yet—and maybe I'll have the tale for you next time I see you."

Penny chuckled. "Paul was right. Horse thieves."

"Or worse."

"You really enjoy this kind of thing, don't you?"

A shadow came over Cathy's eyes. "It keeps me busy. You have your dreams of turn-of-the-century towns; I have my stacks of dusty reference books and yellowed newspapers." Suddenly her eyes widened. "Oh, my God. I wonder if . . ." She quickly unfolded the sheaf of papers from her purse and began scanning through them.

"What?" Penny demanded.

Cathy hushed her with a raised hand. And in a moment she said, without looking up, "Did you say one of those names was Hamlin?"

"What?"

"From your dream."

"Oh. Yes, I think I did. Myra Hamlin and Netty Baker and Jenny Fowler. All women. That's funny."

"Hamlin, Henry C.," Cathy said, pointing with her fingernail to a line on the Xeroxed page. "Owned a house in Mercy which he inherited from his father in 1892; still lived there when the house was destroyed by the flood of 1928."

"There are a lot of Hamlins, Cathy."

"Lived there," Cathy repeated for emphasis, "with his wife Myra."

Penny snatched the paper from her. "Let me see that."

Her eyes scanned the listing Cathy had just read, and went on to search for Baker, Netty, and Fowler, Jenny.

"What do you know about that?" she said softly. " 'Netty Baker, who ran the post office from the time of her husband's death in 1918 until her own demise in 1930.' Now, how in the world do you suppose I could have known about that?"

"Did you ever hear of the collective unconscious?"

Penny made a face, searching down the rows of names. "I don't think that theory was designed to cover dreams about people who've been dead for seventy years."

"Why not? You dream you've gone back in time; why *wouldn't* you dream about the people who were alive then?"

Penny handed the papers back to her. "No Jenny Fowler."

"That just means she didn't still live there when the lake was built. She could have died, or moved away, or married and changed her name."

Penny's expression was noncommittal.

"Oh, come on, Penny! You can't tell me you're not just a little bit blown away by this!"

She shrugged. "I heard the names someplace. Maybe I even saw this book of yours, back when Paul and I were first poking around the area. It was a long time ago; I've probably forgotten half of what we picked up about the house and the community back then. We couldn't even remember the name of the town the other night at dinner."

"You are such a wet blanket. Wouldn't it be fun to have a good mystery in your life? Do you have to have an explanation for everything?"

And Penny answered simply, "Yes."

"You should tell Elsie about your dream, though. If she's

interested in the way things used to be, she'd love thinking her mother has actually *seen* it. After all, everyone loves a good ghost story."

Penny made a face. "I don't think so. She's one person who does have enough mysteries in her life." She turned over the check and reached for her purse.

"Sorry," Cathy said. "I guess you're right." She took the check from Penny. "My turn. You think it's okay to give her the papers, though, right? It didn't occur to me to ask you about it."

Penny smiled. "Of course it's okay. I'm glad she has a project. And I'm glad to have you for a friend. Thanks for today, Cat. You don't know how much it means to me to be able to not think about things for a while. Now, what can I do for you?"

Cathy took out some bills from her purse and laid them atop the check, then looked up at Penny with a wan smile. "Tell me I'm not going to be a widow at forty-two?"

Penny reached across the table and squeezed her hand, and they sat there in silence until the moment passed.

Then Cathy said, "I like not thinking about things too." And she forced a smile. "So let me have my mysteries and my ghost stories, okay? Maybe Elsie and I have more in common than we realized."

Penny smiled back. "You got it, sweetie. And when I get back home and realize I saw this whole dream on a movie-of-the-week, I promise not to tell you, okay?"

"Now, that's a friend. And I promise not to ever let on to your daughter that you might, just possibly, have a little bit of imagination left in that scientifically sterilized brain of yours."

They walked together across the street to meet Elsie, and true to her word, Cathy did not mention the dream again.

ELEVEN

Is it possible to grieve twice for what is lost? I tell you it is possible to grieve a thousand times, to grieve for a hundred thousand years, to lose yourself in grief, to drown in its great whirling undertow and be sucked to the bottom of a bottomless chasm of grief; oh, yes, it is possible.

Before I ever found my way home, I had known my family was gone, and Michael had confirmed it. Yet hope is such a wicked, desperate thing, and even knowing the truth could not ease the pain of knowing it was true. These people were not my family. This was a girl named Elsie Marie and a man named Paul Mason, and they had nothing to do with me. Nothing.

I was angry. Not so much for my loss, though that was part of it, but because now suddenly, once again, nothing made sense. Why was this incredible, peculiar, and utterly impossible thing happening to me if not to guide me back to my lost family? I had lost my memory, my sense of identity, my purpose; all that was left to me was this strange miracle and the hope that it might somehow make whole what was broken in my life.

And yet it was a vain hope. There was no purpose to these random glimpses into a fractured world, no grand scheme to this aberration in time and space. It was . . . pointless. For isn't that what we all seek, essentially, the only thing—order from chaos? Once I had it; once there was a pattern, a reason, a method. Now there was only chaos. And I was in despair.

I stood in the parlor, looking again at the photographs that had once so inspired in me memories of my little family, my lost Jeff and my beloved Sarah. But these snapshots, I realized in a slow, dreadful way, were not *my* memories, but those of someone else. The sandy-haired Paul whose face had sparked such instant recognition in me . . . who was he, if not my husband? The darling little girl in the white dress . . . someone else's little girl, not mine. The little girl of the dark-haired woman who laughed into the sun in the photograph, the little girl who had called her Mom . . . but how hard my mind had worked to make myself believe a hope and deny the obvious. These were not my family. They were strangers. And I was as lost as I had ever been.

"I don't believe this."

I turned, and there he was, this Paul who was not my Jeff, this man whose face was so familiar to me and yet that of a stranger. He stood in the doorway of the parlor with an angry scowl on his face, and my senses leapt with surprise. I had thought . . . I don't know why but I had thought that now that I had discovered these people had nothing to do with me I would never see them again, that the miracle of the divided worlds would simply disappear.

How foolish we can be when we imagine we are the center of the universe.

He came toward me purposefully. "Lady, I don't know how you got in here, but I'm telling you right now this is your last chance. I'm going to call the police and file a report and *you*—"

He reached out as though to catch my arm. I stood still. His hand, of course, passed right through me.

He staggered. He stared. He took a stumbling step backward and caught his shin against the edge of a low table. He hardly seemed to notice. He never took his eyes off me, and he said softly, "Holy shit."

I said, "I now see where your daughter gets her language."

I could see the muscles in his throat work as he swallowed. His lips were white at the corners, and the pupils of his eyes enormous. He reached his hand out again, slowly, and carefully tried to close his fingers upon my arm. His hand caught nothing but air, and he jerked it back as though burned.

I said, "I tried to tell you. You're not really here. I'm not really *there* where you see me. Where you are looks like where I am, but it's not."

He seemed to try to make his throat muscles work for several seconds before he actually spoke. "What is this?" He sounded hoarse. "A hologram?" And his eyes began to dart quickly around the room as though he could discern the source of the trick.

"I don't know what that is," I said. "But I don't think so."

"But I'm talking to you," he said slowly, his eyes coming back to me. "There's no such thing as an interactive hologram. How are you doing this?"

"I'm not doing anything. I was just as startled as you are the first time I saw you. And I don't know how you can hear me. No one else can."

"But . . . the other day . . ."

I was growing impatient. "I don't know how it happens. Sometimes I can see you and you can't see me. Sometimes we can see each other. It's like . . . a door opens or something. I don't know why. I don't know when it's going to happen. It's all very confusing."

His eyes were fixed on me, studying my face. "I think I've seen you before, somewhere else. . . . You seem familiar to me."

I tried to ignore the little catch of pain in my heart. "Yes. You seemed familiar to me too. I thought you were . . . but you're not."

He sank back against a tall chair, his hands gripping its back. "This is . . . weird. This is . . . I don't believe this is happening. But it is, isn't it?"

I said, pleading, one last time, "Do you know Jeff? Do you know my Sarah?"

He shook his head. The expression on his face was odd, fixed. "Is that . . . why you're here? To find them?"

And it was my turn to shake my head, in hopelessness and frustration. "I don't know why I'm here! Can't you understand that? I don't know!"

As I spoke, I turned away, looking back with bitterness and yearning at the photographs on the fireplace mantel. I heard him say, "But . . ." and nothing more.

When I looked again, he was gone.

MIRACLE: *a wonderful happening that is contrary to or independent of the known laws of nature; something marvelous, a wonder.*

The actions of a true intellectual, Paul thought. Turning to a book to explain the inexplicable. He closed the dictionary and leaned back in his chair, breathing slowly, deeply. He said aloud again, softly, as he had said for perhaps the dozenth time in the past hour, "Oh, my God, oh, my God."

He should call somebody. Tell somebody. Penny had a one-o'clock surgery; she wouldn't call home before ten. Elsie had gone down to the lake. Who would he tell? *What* would he tell? This was crazy. This was absolutely over-the-top, without-a-damn-doubt, stark-raving crazy, but Jesus, it had *happened*; as plainly and as matter-of-factly as stopping to chat with the postman or opening the fridge for a beer, it had happened. And the excitement that buzzed through his skin and darted and circled inside his brain made him feel alive, purposeful, on the brink, and *potent* in a way he had not felt since . . . ever. He had never felt this way. He had never before held a conversation— three conversations, to be exact—with someone who clearly could not exist.

His thoughts raced through the halls of philosophy and bounced off the walls of doctrine and skidded around the curve of intellect in great tumbling skips and leaps, and he found nothing, *nothing,* that could in any way satisfactorily explain what had just happened to him. *Miracle.* Miracles were something else he did not believe in. God only knew he had stood in need of a miracle more than once in his life, had never expected one, had never received one. Now, all of a sudden . . . this.

Only the very gullible and the very naive believed that there was a reason, or even a moderately explicable purpose, for life's extraordinary events. Yet he, scholar and academic, believer in nothing, kept returning over and over to the question, *Why?*

And the words he kept hearing were, *Don't wreck your marriage, Paul Mason. Please don't do that.*

Incredible. Incredible to believe in apparitions, of course, in disappearing people, in visitations from beyond. More incredible still to think such an event had been sent through space and time to one man in one small town on the face of one small planet in all the universe for the sole purpose of saving his marriage.

A normal man would laugh. Hearing it from anyone else, Paul himself would have laughed. But perhaps the most incredible thing about it was how badly he wanted to believe that what had just happened—what so obviously could not have possibly happened—had indeed taken place. Because whether you believe in miracles or not, he decided, when one happens to you, it changes everything.

IT WAS, Elsie discovered, a lot easier than it was in the movies, and at the same time much more complex.

In a movie, for example—a good one, anyway—she would have gotten the pages from Aunt Cathy, and found a tantalizing bit of information, just enough to confirm that she was on the right track, and the bottom corner of the appropriate page, the one containing the vital detail she desperately needed, would have been torn off or smudged. She then would have taken another route to uncover the truth, and would have discovered the courthouse had burned down or the church records were missing, but there was an old lady in town who remembered . . . and so on.

In fact, it was so simple that Elsie could not understand why Aunt Cathy hadn't already figured it out, until she remembered that her aunt had a great deal more on her mind these days than genealogy.

The 1932 property owners of the communities of Mercy, Abercrombe Parcel, and Riverwalk—the three adjoining riverside villages that had been swallowed up or made uninhabitable by the lake, were listed in alphabetical order. There were sixty-two altogether, with the greatest concentration of them—forty-six—being in Mercy. Apparently Mercy was the center of activity for the three little towns, with its own post office, general store, doctor, and dentist, as well as a number of other small businesses and two churches, a Methodist and a Baptist.

It took Elsie a little while to figure out the format, but no time at all to find what she was looking for. On the next-to-the-last page, right in the middle, there it was: *Mason, John Edward of Logantown, North Carolina, received $120 for a two-story frame house with solid porches on two acres of land located three hundred feet from the river on the southwest corner of Liberty Street in Mercy, North Carolina.*

John Mason inherited the house in 1923 from his parents, Nelson and Maryanne Mason . . .

There Elsie had to stop, her heart pounding so hard that the words actually strobed before her eyes, *Maryanne. Mary . . .* She had expected it, yes; she had hoped she was right, been almost certain she was right. But to actually see it there in black-and-white photocopied print from some dull and utterly trustworthy account book . . . that was something else. It took her breath away. It was a moment before she could focus again.

Nelson and Maryanne Mason, who inherited it from Nelson's father, Winston Mason. Though the house was originally purchased for destruction, it turned out to be one of the twelve left unmolested when the engineers redesigned the dam.

"Yes," Elsie whispered triumphantly. She *had* to be right. It was all just too perfect.

But two things struck her. First, she couldn't believe the price—$120—someone had paid for a house and two acres in

1932. Wouldn't her dad bust a gut over that one? And second, why was John Edward Mason—her great-grandfather—living in Logantown when his house was here? She remembered her dad saying that his folks were from around Logantown, but how had they ended up there? If the building of the dam and the lake had driven them away, John Edward would not have been listed as being "of Logantown" before the lake was built. Would he?

As for the rest of the mystery, all she had to do was go to the phone book. The not-very-good watercolor by some local artist depicting an aerial view of how the tri-community area would have looked/might have looked at the turn of the century. A snaky blue river meandered around the border of the painting, while landmarks were depicted with two-dimensional church steeples and storefronts with FEED AND SEED or MER-CANTILE on them, and miniature doll people walked the streets in their odd, old-fashioned clothes. The streets were lined with circular green trees and bushes, and little square houses with gas lanterns and cobblestone paths, and every street had a sign. From the southwest corner of Liberty Street the post office was at a thirty-degree angle and less than four blocks away.

On the inside cover of the phone book was a modern-day map of the area, including the lake, the highway, the new roads that had been built—some paved, some not—to accommodate the slow but steady growth of the past quarter century. The road they lived on was barely worth a squiggle on the map, but she did find it. And she found the old post office at the corner of Route 1 and County Road 10. The angle that she drew from that corner to the squiggle that was their dirt road was approximately thirty degrees. And it couldn't have been more than four village blocks away as the crow flies.

"Bingo," she said out loud, her heart pounding. "Dad, old man, not only did you return to the land of your ancestors; you're living in his freaking *house*."

I THINK I MAY HAVE BEEN SLEEPING; time had begun to do that odd blending-together thing again, as it had done when I first came home. I think there were long periods of time when I was awake that I did not remember being awake, and when I slept it sometimes seemed I slept for days. Perhaps my condition was worsening, and perhaps I should have been alarmed. But I did not care. In truth, I did not care about very much of anything at all.

At any rate, I came awake in my room and I saw him there, the man called Paul, moving across the floor in a very purposeful way and kneeling beside a small door in the corner of the room where the sloped ceiling almost met the floor. Odd. I had never noticed that little door before.

He seemed unaware of me, and I just watched him, quietly and with a detached interest, as he pulled open the door and dragged out a cardboard box. He started taking things out. A dusty sandalwood box with a tattered velvet lining. Some scraps of lace. A riding crop. A silver buttonhook and a cloth bag containing what appeared to be mismatched pieces of costume jewelry. These he discarded quickly and without much interest. And then he came to the tin box filled with photographs.

There was a peculiar feeling in my chest as he opened that tin box. I wanted a closer look. I drew slowly closer.

Then the door to the room opened and Sarah—no, not Sarah, the child Elsie—came in. Or she started to come in; then she stopped cold when she saw her father. She was not my Sarah but was so like my child would have been, might have been, so much like the child I yearned to have, that my heart ached with just the sight of her. Oh, why couldn't they both just go away and leave me alone? Why must I be so continually tormented with scraps of their petty and unimportant little lives?

She did not appear to notice me either. Her eyes were fixed on Paul. "What," she said, in a voice like ice, "are you doing in my room?"

He barely glanced over his shoulder. "Looking for some stuff I remember finding up here when we remodeled the attic space. Old pictures and things, from the previous owners of the house, I guess. I meant to get them out and show them to your mom, but what with one thing or another, I forgot." He spoke distractedly, turning over photographs, looking for something.

Elsie strode over to him angrily. "That doesn't give you any right to come barging in my room when I'm not here, searching through my stuff—"

"It's not your stuff; it's not even my stuff. Who knows who it belongs to. Jeez, some of these pictures have got to be fifty years old. Look at that top hat."

"Why don't you just take your stupid box of stuff and—"

She stopped suddenly as Paul turned over another photograph. So did he. They both stared.

I was looking at a picture of myself, young, beautiful, in a new lilac suit and my best Sunday hat. The colors in the photograph were all browns and oranges, but I knew the suit was lilac and the hat had a veil of ivory trimmed in hand-stitched lavender embroidery. I stood with my hands primly together on the lawn in front of the Baptist church, unsmiling, unblinking, staring straight at the camera as I had been told.

Elsie whispered, "Oh, my God. It's her."

Paul whipped his head around, staring at his daughter. He seemed to speak before he planned to. "You've seen her too?"

Their eyes met and an entire stream of unspoken emotions seemed to pass between them. But all Elsie responded was, "A lot." Her voice sounded tight, strangulated in her throat. "I've seen her a lot."

The straightness seemed to go out of Paul's spine and he sank back on his heels. The hand that held the photograph dropped to his lap. "Jesus," he said. "Jesus."

Elsie came and knelt beside him, taking the photograph, studying it. "Her name is Mary," she said.

"I knew I had seen her before," Paul said. "I knew it. I just couldn't remember where." He looked at his daughter. "She *said* she knew you. Remember, I told you that night at dinner? But I didn't know then that she was . . . Oh, my God this is unbelievable."

Elsie said, "She talked to you? Are you kidding me—she talked to you?"

Paul said, "This photograph has to be seventy years old at least. That church—it was one of the first things to be torn down in 1932. She looks like she's about twenty in the photograph. That would make her, what? Ninety years old?"

Elsie looked up at him. "Dad," she said slowly, "the woman in this picture has been dead since 1923."

REMEMBERING

TWELVE

"You lied to me!" I cried furiously. "From the very beginning, everything you've said to me, all the answers to my questions, they've been lies, nothing but lies! No, don't touch me; don't look at me!" I backed away, flinging up my hands to ward Michael off as he approached. "How can you even face me after what you've done? How can you face yourself?"

Michael said calmly, "What have I done?"

"Everything!" I screamed at him. And, "Nothing! You've done nothing to help me, nothing to guide me; you've let me believe whatever fantasy came to mind. . . ." I caught in a ragged breath. "I am not dead," I said with conviction. *"This"*— I gestured to include myself, my surroundings, even him—"is not what dead feels like."

"What does dead feel like?" he inquired.

I believe in the resurrection and life through Christ our Lord. I pressed my hands to my ears, hard, to blot out the words in my head, and I shouted at him, "Not like this! It doesn't feel like this!"

I drew a quick, sharp breath and I flung out my hands, squaring my shoulders, prepared to take on the world and all his persuasion. "Death is different. It isn't walking in the garden and dozing by the window and . . . and having conversations with people in your parlor! It isn't waking and sleeping, eating and drinking and . . . and thinking and wondering; it just isn't!"

He inquired reasonably, "Why not?"

I simply stared at him.

"Why couldn't it be exactly what you've just described? Why couldn't it be whatever you imagine?"

"Because," I cried. *I believe in the resurrection and the life . . .* "Because it's not!"

"Think about it." His tone was calm and persuasive. "In the beginning, what details do you remember of your life at home? Weren't your days painted in broad and general strokes? Where were the details?"

"There were details," I returned angrily. "There was the lamp, and the stove I couldn't work. . . ." There I faltered a little, remembering how odd it seemed that I had had so little power over these common things. But I rallied determinedly. "And the frog, the stone frog in the garden . . ." A garden without roses. *I believe in the resurrection . . .* "And Je— Paul, that man Paul, in my house! He knows I'm real. He's talked to me; we've talked to each other. Ask him, if you don't believe me!"

All I saw in his eyes was sympathy, and I turned angrily away. "They are the ones who're dead, then, those people in my house; if anyone isn't real it's them. *They're* the ghosts; I've always known that, even when I thought they were . . . when I thought they were . . ."

I turned to him, unable to keep the despair from my eyes or my voice. "They're gone, aren't they? My Jeff and my Sarah. They're gone and I can't get them back and it's all my fault."

"No," he said gently. "They're not gone."

I clapped my hands to my ears. "No more lies! Why did you let me hope? Why did you let me think I might be able to reach them; why did you let me think I could save them?"

He said quietly, "You are the only one who can save them."

"Stop it! Just stop it!" And I sank to my knees with my hands over my ears, weeping bitterly.

"Mary, listen to me." He knelt beside me, and I felt his hands over mine, prying my fingers from my ears. "Do you remember when you first woke up; do you remember what you wanted? You wanted your life back, you wanted to remember, you wanted to go home. I promised I would help you and I will. But you can't give up now; you have to help me."

"You sent me home to a house filled with ghosts! Everything I remember is wrong. You haven't helped me at all, not at all."

"Do you really believe they're ghosts, Mary?"

"I don't care what they are! I want them gone; I never want to see them again. I just want to be left alone!"

He touched my face, making me look at him. "Mary, think about this for a moment. What if this *is* what death is like? Just consider it. What if you were right the first time and there are many, many worlds filled with many lives, ordinary lives and grand lives, where we wake and sleep and work and play and do great things and small, good things and bad . . . and what if to die in one world is only to be born into another?"

His gaze was so dear, so gentle, so intense and compelling, that I felt it drawing me in, sweeping me away, making me believe.

"And what if," he continued, his fingers tight on mine, "occasionally, through some great miracle, those worlds intersect, and the lives in one world can affect the lives in another. What if that is what has happened to you?"

I shook my head slowly, hardly aware of the denial I spoke, it was so soft. "No. No."

He took my hands in a firm and solid grip. "Mary," he said in a firm tone, "Look around you. What do you see?"

I looked at him; I looked beyond him, and I saw . . . nothing. No walls, no floor, no chairs or tables, just a clear white light. Nothing else at all.

It was a long time before I could speak. Then I said in a tone that was as flat and dry as I felt inside, "You did that. How did you do that?"

He just looked at me in silence and long, steady patience.

"You've been doing this to me all along!" I accused dully. "None of this has been real, none of it. It's all been a dream that you've somehow made me believe." And at that moment, knowing it was gone, I longed for nothing more in my life than to have the threads of that dream woven back together again, to immerse myself in it and pretend it was my life.

He said gently, "I've done nothing. You have. Don't you see, Mary, nothing is real until you make it so."

"Stop your riddles; they're driving me mad! How can I know what it's like to be dead," I cried, "when I can't even remember what it's like to be alive?"

Still he said nothing.

"I am not dead," I insisted loudly, firmly, albeit a bit unsteadily. "They are the ghosts. *They're* the ghosts!"

"Mary," he said gently. "What does it matter?"

"They are not my family," I said shakily. "I want them to go away. They have nothing to do with me."

"They have everything to do with you; you must understand that. You can't just wish them away."

Again he held me with his gaze, his strong and certain gaze, pleading for my understanding. "Mary, this world in which you've lived since you awoke is not where you belong. Don't you see it's not real? You have a life waiting for you as real as the one Paul and Elsie and Penny have, a life where people love you and where you'll continue to learn and grow and live and laugh every day. And the only thing keeping you from the life you are supposed to be living right now is yourself."

"I believe in Christ our Lord," I whispered, like a talisman. "I believe in the resurrection and the life . . ."

He smiled. "So do I."

I pulled away from him with swift, hard strength. "Maybe you're evil. You're the devil and you're trying to convince me of monstrous lies."

The smile did not fade. "I am not."

I released a long, tired breath, and everything within me seemed to sag, weighing down my spirit. "I know."

And with an effort I focused on him. "Then answer me this. What is the reason? Why has this happened to me? And the man, Paul—why is he the only one who can hear me? He has nothing to say, but he can hear me."

"He's the key. He's the one who's keeping you here. They all are, really."

"What happened to my family?" I demanded.

"Nothing. They're waiting for you in that other life, but you have to be ready to go to them."

"I'm ready!" I cried. "Take me to them!"

He shook his head slowly. "In your heart you know I can't. You have to find them on your own."

I wanted to weep and weep and weep, but I was so very tired, and growing more tired by the moment. I could hardly keep my thoughts focused, the words coherent.

"What happened to them? What did I do to them? Why can't I remember . . . ?"

"That's why you have to go back, to Paul and Elsie and Penny."

"No. I'm never going back. They are not my family and they have nothing to do with me."

"They are as much your family as any you've ever known."

"No." The word was part whisper, part moan. "No, I'm not doing this anymore; I'm not listening to you. It's not real, none of it, and I can wish them away if I want to. You told me so."

"Mary, if you give up now you'll never remember. You'll never have your life back."

"I'm tired. I'm so tired. I just want to sleep. Leave me alone. Just let me sleep."

"Don't do this," he begged. "Don't let us lose you again. Mary, please . . ."

But his voice sounded farther and farther away, words blurring and finally dissolving into a low, pleasant hum. I closed my eyes, and remembered nothing more.

And then he said, "Think of Sarah. . . ."

PAUL SAID, "When did you first see her?"

They were on the front porch with the meager contents of the box spread out on the painted board floor between them. The afternoon was sultry, thick with the sound of droning bees and the faraway putt of an outboard motor far up the lake. It was as though the hugeness of their discovery, and the excitement it generated, was too much to be contained within four walls, so they had moved outside. They had not stopped talking since finding the picture.

Elsie picked up a small onyx broach, looked at it for what must have been the tenth time, and put it down again. "I guess not long after we got here. Of course, I didn't know it was her. I mean, I didn't know it was anything except some trespasser. I wonder if she wore this." She fingered the broach again.

"Not all of the stuff in this box is from the same period. Here are some canceled checks from 1935. Funny the things people save."

"Tell me what she said to you again."

"She wanted to know when they built the lake. I should have known something was strange then. She seemed to be looking for someone. . . ."

"Her family," Elsie said quickly.

"Maybe," Paul hedged. "And the first time . . . well, she seemed to think I was someone else. Then she was disappointed that I wasn't."

"You mean you talked to her more than once?" Elsie's eyes were big.

So Paul recounted, in as much detail as he could, the encounters with the mysterious woman in the photograph. He left out her plea to save his marriage; some things were simply personal. But he thought about it. And every time he did, his heart beat faster.

"What's weird is," Elsie said, "you could hear her and I couldn't. Why do you suppose that is? I mean, she was trying to talk to me, only it was like there was soundproof glass or something between us. And the other thing is, she seemed as surprised to see me as I was to see her. And if she is dead, how could she write her name on my window, and dig up that stone frog in the yard?"

Paul stared at his daughter. "She did that?"

Elsie nodded vigorously. "The other night in my room I just looked up and she was there! She was trying to tell me something but I couldn't hear her. So I asked her to write her name with a pen, but I guess she couldn't do that because she looked really sad when I asked her to, and then she went over to the window and wrote her name in the fog. Mary. No last name."

"And then?"

"Then she just wasn't there anymore."

Paul released a breath, and sat back on his heels. "Wow."

"Yeah. And right before that was when I saw her digging in the yard. When I went over there, there was this piece of a frog statue that had been dug up. I mean, how can a dead person do that?"

Again a soft release of breath. "She shouldn't be able to. Elsie, why didn't you tell me any of this?"

She looked briefly uncomfortable, and shrugged. "I tried to a couple of times, believe it or not. Remember when I asked about the voices?"

He looked blank.

"Sometimes you can hear them, people talking back and forth, and pots and pans rattling and teakettles whistling. In the kitchen mostly. You've never heard them?"

He shook his head slowly. "What do they say?"

She was thoughtful. "Just stuff. About what they're having for dinner and what they're planning to do that day, nothing interesting." And then she looked wary. "Why? Do you think that sounds crazy?"

He shook his head slowly. "Honey, I just had two rather bizarre conversations with a woman who has to be over ninety, if she's alive at all, and who I could have sworn was still in her twenties. I won't be using the word 'crazy' to describe anyone for a long time."

Elsie grinned. "It's funny, isn't it? We almost never talk about stuff, and look what it took to get us talking."

He smiled back at her. "Yeah. Look what it took." And because the love and wonder in his eyes were so intense, so overwhelming, that he was sure they would embarrass her and ruin the moment, he broke eye contact first, busying himself with the scraps of paper on the floor. "You'd think there would be something useful in all this junk. A wedding announcement, a birth notice, something with a name and date."

"Maybe she's in another dimension," Elsie suggested. "And maybe every now and then her dimension intersects with this one, and that's how she's able to talk and move things and stuff."

"There are a lot of things science can't explain," Paul admitted cautiously.

"Or maybe she *is* dead, and being dead doesn't mean what we thought it does. Why do you suppose she would come back now? To us?"

Again Paul was very cautious. "I don't know. I think . . ." But he looked into his daughter's eager, alert eyes and finished simply, "I think we need more information."

"How can we get it?" she demanded.

He couldn't help smiling. "Well, we might have to scour the historical records all over the state. But your mom's gone for the rest of the week, and with the two of us working on it . . . I don't see why we shouldn't give it a try, do you?"

Elsie held up her hand for a high five, and Paul slapped his palm against it. He knew there were very few purely perfect moments in one's life that were recognized when they occurred and were revered when they were past, and that he had just experienced one of them. It was the kind of moment that could change everything.

And he had a ghost to thank.

IN HER DREAM, Penny heard no sound. No screams, no sobs, no crashing movements or ragged breaths. It was like a movie with the sound turned off, only she felt the warm splatter of blood across her face, smelled its iron as it pooled on the floor beside her. She saw the footprints, the bloody footprints that were left from heavy black boots as they moved across the floor, searching, stalking. She could feel her own fear, a terror so absolute it had a taste, bitter and cold on the back of her throat, and she thought she would die of fear, that her heart would burst of the dread of waiting, waiting for him to find her. And she hated herself because people were dying and all she could think of was her own fear, of what was going to happen to her, she was consumed with it; she was paralyzed with it; she was nothing but fear.

And then he was there. She saw the bloody hand and the flash of the blade, and then she saw the face. And when she opened her mouth to scream no sound would come out.

Penny awoke on an indrawn, choking breath, and she was in her own bed at home in Chapel Hill, alone. Her heart was pounding in her chest and she had to lie there a moment, breathing hard, orienting herself.

She was not in the kitchen of the lake house. She had dreamed it all. She had stayed over in town because she had a heavy caseload this week, and she wasn't at the lake house at all. There was no blood in the kitchen. None.

She swung her legs over the side of the bed and sat there, the skin on her legs prickling in the artificially cooled air beneath the hem of her nightshirt. She gripped the side of the bed and took several more deep breaths. *I'm losing it,* she thought. *I think I'm really losing it.*

In fact, her caseload hadn't been any heavier this week than another. It was simply becoming harder and harder to go back to the lake house.

She got out of bed and went over to the chaise, where she had left her bag and her raincoat and the package she had picked up on the way home last night. She had been too tired to look at it, but now she undid the brown-paper wrapping and pulled out the shrink-wrapped print.

It had been absurdly easy to find. It turned out the artist was quite well known for his depictions of small North Carolina towns in earlier times, and the second gallery she had called carried his prints. She gazed at the brightly colored painting, the church, the livery that wasn't a livery, the post office, the elm trees. Here would be Jenny Fowler's house, and there would be Myra Hamlin, and over there . . . But try as she might, she could not wash away the stain of the nightmare with the sweet memories of an earlier dream. All she could see was blood. Blood and the dripping hand that held the blade, and the face that belonged to that hand.

She put the painting down abruptly and went to the bathroom, where she knelt beside the toilet and began to retch.

*   *   *

"I HOPE YOU DON'T MIND doing this over lunch," Mike Turner said as he slid into the chair across from her.

"What, are you kidding? If I didn't do consultations over lunch I would never eat lunch." Penny took the menu the hostess offered and opened it.

"Same here all too often, I'm afraid."

They chatted for a while about neutral subjects, and colleagues they had in common, and gave their orders. Then Mike said, "How is life at the lake?"

She could feel the shadow cross her face and did not know how to cover it, so she tried to minimize it. "Well, it's difficult, with the commute and all. I'm not getting to spend as much time there as I would like. Paul has done all this remodeling and . . . well, it's just not like it used to be." She couldn't believe she was chatting on so aimlessly when a simple "Fine" would have sufficed. She took a drink of water to silence herself.

But he did not appear to notice her nervousness—or, more likely, he was professional enough to keep it from showing. He merely smiled and said, "Few things are. What have you done to the house?"

"What?"

"You said Paul had done some remodeling."

"Oh. He ripped out the kitchen, gutted the attic, and tore out the back wall to enlarge the bedroom. It's really nice." *Rip, gut, tear.* Even she could not fail to notice the violence in the choice of words, and she couldn't get that vision of the bloodied knife out of her head.

"You should pardon me for saying so, but you don't sound as though it's very nice."

She drew in and released a long breath. "Mike," she said, "I know you're not being paid to hear this, but I don't think I'm going to be able to save my marriage." There. The words were out. She hadn't really even thought them before, but now they were spoken and they had been shockingly easy to say.

"I'm so sorry." The sympathy in his voice, and in his eyes, was genuine.

Her throat felt hot and tight, and she shifted her eyes away momentarily to avoid the sting of tears. When she spoke it was only a hoarse, "Yeah. Me too."

"You know I'd be glad to have the two of you come in, if you think it would help."

He looked so genuinely concerned that she forced a smile and a nod. "Thanks. I'll talk to Paul."

"One of the saddest things about my job is having to watch families fall apart just when they need each other most. There've been enough victims in this situation already. I'd hate to see your family become another one."

She tried to make her expression wry, but suspected it looked only sad. "The funny thing is, I think if this had happened ten years ago we could have survived it better. We were different people then. Not necessarily stronger, just . . . different."

"In what way?"

She lifted a shoulder, pleating a paper napkin with her fingers. "In lots of ways. We were more open to possibilities. More hopeful, maybe. And we could talk about anything. I mean, we used to spend hours discussing things like astral projection and kinesthetic clairvoyance and life after death; can you believe that? I mean seriously discussing it. Now we can't even talk about what to have for dinner without getting into a fight." She sighed. "Cathy says I have no imagination, but I wasn't always that way. I think that Paul has all but lost his, and maybe that's my fault. But somehow, over the years, we've lost our ability to . . . I don't know, believe in the impossible, I guess. And I'm afraid that one of those impossible things we no longer believe in is marriage."

"Maybe," suggested Mike, "if you could find a way to connect with the people you used to be, you could also find a way to connect with each other."

"Well, that's the trick, isn't it?" She smiled wanly. "Figuring out how to do that."

He took up his coffee. "No trick to it, really. The hard part is deciding whether or not you want to."

She didn't know what to say to that. She didn't even know what to think. So she took another breath and squared her shoulders. "Thanks for listening, Mike. Now, what about Elsie?"

He leaned back in his chair. "Well, I'd be happier if she were showing some signs of remembering by now. There haven't been any major changes, but I did want to alert you to the upcoming anniversary date, which can often precipitate a crisis. How is she doing at home?"

"A little better, I think, more communicative. And she's gotten interested in this genealogy thing, which is good. We talked about her going to school in the fall. She wasn't crazy about the idea, but at least we talked."

He nodded. "Keep that line of communication open. If she misses starting school with the other kids, it will only make it twice as hard later."

Penny's beeper vibrated in silent mode against her belt. She glanced down at it. "It's the hospital," she apologized, and took out her cell phone.

She dialed the number, identified herself, and listened for a few minutes to the voice on the other end. Then she said, "Tell her I'll be there in ten minutes." And flipped the phone shut.

"Mike, I'm sorry," she said, sliding out of her chair. "Can we do this later? My brother-in-law has just been taken to the ER, and I need to be there."

But he was already on his feet, waving her on.

"I'M SORRY; I shouldn't have called; it's just there was so much blood—"

"It's okay." Penny took her friend in a one-armed embrace, rubbing her shoulder soothingly. "It was just a ruptured blood vessel in his esophagus. I know it looks scary, but it's not all that uncommon during radiation therapy. They're calling in Dr. Pitman, and you'll feel better after he checks everything out. But I promise you, this is not a crisis. He's okay."

Cathy wiped her face with the back of her hand, smearing tears. "As okay as you can be when you're dying, I guess." And then she shuddered and made a little choking sound, as though trying to smother a memory. "There was blood all over the bathroom floor. I tried to mop it up with a towel before the ambulance got there. I don't know what I was thinking. There was just so much of it."

All over the kitchen floor, Penny thought, *dripping down the cabinets, splattered on my clothes . . .* But then she noticed the actual blood smears on Cathy's sleeves and the hem of her khaki pants, and she brought herself abruptly back to the present.

"Come over here; sit down." She guided Cathy firmly to a sofa and sat beside her. "You'll be able to see him in a few minutes, and then you're coming home with me for the night."

"No, I want to stay. I've done it before. That big chair in the corner makes into a bed."

"I called Paul."

"You told him not to come, didn't you?" Cathy looked anxious, and Penny patted her hand reassuringly.

"I told him Andrew would probably be coming home in the morning. He'll call the room later."

"Good." Her voice was tired. "I don't want to wear out everyone's goodwill before I really need it."

"You're not going to wear out our goodwill, Cathy. What a thing to say."

"You know what I mean. Things are only going to get worse."

Penny had nothing to say to that. Long ago she had promised Cathy she would not soothe her—or herself—with meaningless platitudes and slim false hopes. It might make Penny feel better as a medical professional to say, "There's still a chance" or "He's responding well to treatment," but in face of the truth it was nothing but cruel.

Cathy took a long, slow breath, calming herself, and stretched out her fingers. "I need you to recommend a hospice for me, Penny."

Penny was silent for a moment, considering and rejecting one selfish protest after another. Finally she said, "Has Andrew decided to discontinue treatment then?"

Cathy nodded her head. It was a creaky, hesitant movement, as though even the necessity for it caused her pain. "Even before this"—and she made a faint, wry expression—"noncrisis, we talked about things . . . between us, I mean. He's so sick, Penny. The tumor isn't responding at all; if anything, it seems to be growing, and he doesn't want to spend whatever time is left like this. I want him to live forever, but how can I ask him to go through this when we know . . . when we know what the likely outcome will be?" She paused to take a couple of steadying breaths. "We were going to talk to Dr. Pitman on Wednesday, but Andrew's mind is made up."

Penny fought down the doctor in her and tried to think only like a friend. She said at last, very quietly, "I can't imagine how difficult that conversation must have been for you. It must have broken you in half to agree. I'm not sure I could have done it."

Cathy smiled weakly. "Yes," she said, "you could have. I just wish . . ." But she dropped her gaze, and didn't finish.

"Wish what?"

Cathy did not look up. She said softly, "I love him so much, Penny. And death is so permanent."

A picture of Paul came into Penny's mind, and her throat was filled with an aching lump that threatened to cut off her breath. Just Paul with paint splattered on his jeans and sunshine in his hair and a look of intense concentration on his face as he painted a careful corner on the front porch, a simple thing, just Paul. Why that memory, of all the others she had accumulated over the years, should come to the fore to break her heart now she could not say, but she knew that what she felt when she thought of him was as intense now as it had been when they were in college, and that it wasn't going to go away anytime soon. She wasn't ready to say good-bye to Paul, any more than Cathy was ready to say good-bye to Andrew. The difference was, she had a choice.

Penny leaned over and hugged Cathy. "We're here for you, honey," she said. "Both of us."

"I hope so," Cathy whispered.

The two women moved apart and Cathy fumbled in her purse for a tissue. She wiped her eyes and spent a few moments repairing her face. "What a mess I am," she said, and this time her smile seemed less forced, though weary and wan. "I've definitely got to get it together before things get really tough."

"I think you're doing pretty great now."

"You might be a little prejudiced." She sniffed into a tissue and pressed it again briefly and firmly to her eyes. Then, as though putting a firm punctuation mark to her emotions, she straightened her shoulders, drew a breath, and sat back. "It's so funny. I was going to call you this afternoon anyway. I found this book on the history of lost North Carolina towns I thought Elsie might like. It's got a whole chapter on Mercy. As a matter of fact, I didn't even get a chance to take it out of my purse before . . ." She didn't have to finish the sentence. Instead she busied herself with reaching into her oversize bag and drawing out a book with a faded blue cover. She flipped through the pages.

"The weird thing is I found it by doing a search for 'Mason, Winston'—you know, that ancestor of ours I told you about who used to live in Mercy. I thought he was forced to leave because of some scandal, remember?"

Penny followed Cathy's lead. She had known Cathy too long and loved her too well not to be sensitive to what she needed and when she needed it. She nodded and pretended interest.

"Well, just look at this chapter heading." She turned the book around so that Penny could read the caption: *Brutality and Murder in Mercy*.

Penny lifted an eyebrow. "I'm not sure I want Elsie reading that."

"That's why I thought you'd want to look at it first. I was going to, but . . . well, I guess I'm not much in the mood tonight. But Penny, listen to this. The opening: 'Winston Mason was a gentle man, a good husband and father, according to his neighbors. He worked as an accounting clerk at the general store in Mercy, North Carolina, where he had been born and raised. . . .' "

Cathy looked up at Penny. "It's all about him, Penny. Our ancestor. And it's starting to look as though it wasn't scandal that drove him out of Mercy at all. It was murder."

THIRTEEN

"But how will I know when I'm grown up?" asked the boy. "Easy," replied the dog. "When you're grown up you won't be able to hear me anymore."

— *The Boy Who Could Speak Dog,* Paul Mason

Paul said, "Well, that's it, then. The house the Masons owned burned down in 1940. It couldn't possibly be the one we're living in now."

The Wilmington County Historical Society had been a surprisingly accessible, albeit somewhat disorganized, source of information. It had taken Paul and Elsie two trips and approximately six hours of digging through dusty boxes of photocopied records to find the land deeds of the lost lake towns, and then they had barely held out hope that the records would go back beyond the building of the lakes. But they had.

When Elsie grudgingly admitted that her dad had a knack for this kind of research that she herself would have never been able to master, Paul felt a surge of pride that even the National Book Award could not rival. He could not stop the recurring sense of amazement over the fact that he and his daughter were engaged in a project for which they shared such an absorption, working as a team, relating as equals. It was a gift unlike any he had ever imagined, and of all the unbelievable things he had encountered in the past few days, this was the most miraculous, and the most precious.

They had stayed up all night after discovering the photograph, talking about the ghost, possible explanations for the ghost, how each of them felt about the ghost, what could be done about the ghost. They planned and they speculated, they theorized and they confided, and they each knew that no matter what became of this or what happened in the future, their lives, and their relationship, would be forever changed. That was a wondrous thing. A wonderful happening outside the known laws of nature, a marvel. A miracle.

In the past week Paul had completed almost eighty pages of a novel that seemed almost to be writing itself. He was superstitious enough not to invest in a future that might not unfold, but in his heart he knew this was the beginning of the end of the long dry spell, and possibly the germination of something great. It was as though the rusty lock on his imagination had been broken that morning that he opened the box of forgotten mementos and found the photograph of the woman long dead, and a rich cornucopia of fully formed and beautifully interwoven ideas came tumbling out. He had started to believe in possibilities again. He had forgotten how exhilarating that felt.

Elsie said, "But that doesn't make sense. The book says the southwest corner of—"

"Yeah, but look; the way the river bends makes it easy to misread." He pointed with the eraser end of a pencil to a large unfolded plat map that took up most of the space on the library table before them, tracing the corner of the river. "Southwest is this direction here. The Mason house would have been across this street here, where our driveway is now, and down the road a couple of blocks."

"So you're saying . . ." Elsie consulted the fan of deed books that were spread open between them until she found the right one. "The family who owned our house before the lake was built was named Wilcox?"

"Looks like it. Jefferson M. Wilcox, M.D. How about that? He must have been the town doctor. They built the house in 1918. It was purchased by a family named Hayes in 1934, and sold again in 1940, and again in 1952, and so on."

He closed the book, and the two of them spent a few moments thinking about what they had uncovered.

"So we're not related to Mary after all." Elsie sounded disappointed.

"It doesn't look that way."

"But she told you she used to live there," Elsie said thoughtfully. "She said it was her house."

"We still haven't found any actual evidence that anyone named Mary ever lived in Mercy," Paul responded carefully. This was not the time to point out the foolishness of basing their search for the history of the house on the word of a ghost. On the other hand, if not for the ghost, they would not be searching for the history of the house at all.

"Mary *Anne*," Elsie pointed out, "was Nelson Mason's wife."

"Or it could have been Marianne," Paul said. "An entirely different name."

He sat back in the hard armless chair and pushed his hair away from his forehead with his fingers. Every part of him felt sweaty and grimy; even the inside of his mouth felt coated with dust. He looked around the small windowless room and he said, "It's amazing, isn't it? We live in a house that's almost a hundred years old, on the site of what is practically a ghost town—if you'll pardon the expression—and we never even bothered to try to find out its history before. I mean, we wondered about it a lot, and your mom and I used to make up stories about it while we were fixing it up, but we never seriously tried to find out what the *real* story was."

Elsie gave him a crooked little grin. "You'd think a writer would do that, wouldn't you?"

He loved her so much he thought he would burst with it. He wanted to hug her hard and tell her so, but even he was smart enough not to spoil the moment with unsolicited displays of affection from a parent. He said instead, casually, "Did I ever tell you what a great kid you are?"

"Not enough," she answered. Then, "Oh, my God, I can't believe what an idiot I am."

She stood up and withdrew from her jeans pocket a tightly folded, somewhat sweaty and grime-stained sheaf of papers. "What did you say their names were? The people who built our house?"

"Wilcox," he said, understanding. "Does that list your aunt Cathy gave you have the names of the wives, too?"

"Sometimes. And sometimes a little bit about the history of the house." She turned over pages until she got to the last one. "Here it is. Wilcox, Dr. Jefferson Wilcox and his wife . . ." She drew in a soft breath and looked up at him. "Mary." She went on, ". . . and his wife, Mary, built the house in 1919 and lived there until their deaths in 1923." She released a soft breath. "So she *is* dead."

"Wait." Paul sat up straighter. "Didn't you say something else about 1923?"

"That's when John Edward Mason inherited the house from his parents. The house I used to think was ours."

"So his parents must have died in 1923 too. Odd. I wonder if there was a plague or something."

"Could have been."

She returned to the paper in her hand and read on quickly, " 'Built on a gentle hill overlooking the river, the house, which still stands today' "—she cast a quick triumphant look at her father—" 'was the scene of one of the most—' "

She broke off with an expression of disbelief and turned the page over, back again, and over again. "Shit," she said, and Paul winced.

"Come on, Elsie, it's considered bad manners to use profanity in front of your parents. Scene of one of the most what?"

"That's just it. Nothing. Wilcox must have been the last name on the list, and that's all Aunt Cathy copied. It ends there." Then she brightened. "Say! I bet they have this book here!"

But her face fell again as she flipped back through the pages. "Great. The header is cut off on every one of them. Do you have your cell phone? Can you call Aunt Cathy and ask her what the name of the book is?"

He gave her a look. "Honey, I don't think that would be appropriate. She was up all night with Uncle Andrew at the hospital, and I'm not even sure she's home yet. We'll give her a call this evening."

Elsie's lips tightened with frustration. "Well, let's at least ask that old biddy at the desk if she knows about the book."

Paul was beginning to close and stack the books. "You can ask, but I think you'll get a lot further if you don't refer to her as an old biddy. And hurry up; we've got to get going. It's almost noon and I'm starving."

*　　*　　*

ELSIE MET HIM on the street in front of the squat little cracker box that housed the Historical Society with a disappointed look on her face. "She said we should try the university archives."

Paul took out his keys. "Fortunately we have a contact there."

"Jeez, I don't know how you can be so blasé! I mean, here we are on the verge of solving this incredible mystery about our very own house and all you can think about is lunch!"

He unlocked the Explorer with a bleep of the remote-control alarm system, and Elsie opened the passenger-side door. "Speaking of which, what are you in the mood for?"

"Answers."

She slammed the door and he tried not to smile too broadly. He loved seeing her so impassioned about something, anything . . . even this. In this past week he had been given a privileged glimpse into the extraordinary woman she would one day grow to be—so like her mother in so many wonderful ways, and so like himself in as many equally unfortunate ways—and even though he knew they had many years of turbulent adolescence before them in which he would not feel nearly so enthusiastic about her potential, he would never doubt that it was worth the wait.

He got inside and started the engine, adjusting the air-conditioning to quickly cool the stale, hot air. "The mystery—if there is one—will still be there tomorrow, and we have to stop and pick up some groceries before your mom gets home."

She said, "What do you mean, 'if there is one'? We've got a ghost, for God's sake! How much more mysterious do you want it to get?"

Paul was very, very carefully quiet. He could feel her

watching him, and he could feel all the good things that had developed between them over the past week teetering on the edge of dissolution.

Several silent miles passed between them. Then Elsie said, "Why haven't you told Mom?"

"What?"

"About the ghost. You've talked to her every night. You never mentioned it."

He kept his eyes on the road. "You've talked to her too. Why didn't you tell her?"

She shrugged. "You guys are married. You're not supposed to keep secrets from each other. Are you?"

Trust a thirteen-year-old to drive the knife home. He said, walking on eggshells, "It's not exactly the kind of thing you talk about over the phone."

"You think she won't believe you."

Okay, thought Paul, *try to explain to your thirteen-year-old daughter why her mother has no reason to believe anything you say, and why telling her something like this, even in passing, would make her go ballistic, and why you don't want to shatter this fragile, wonderful secret fantasy you've shared with the intrusion of the truth, even when that truth wears the face of her mother.*

He said carefully, "Maybe I'm jealous."

"Of what?"

"Of you. Of our time together. Of our secret."

"Nice try."

"It's the truth."

"Maybe. But maybe more of the truth is you don't want to tell Mom because she'll say I'm crazy." Elsie's tone was matter-of-fact. "And that you're being irresponsible for encouraging me. Don't defend her; she can't help being her."

It was only getting worse. "I don't like you talking that way about your mother. Besides, it's not that simple."

"Why not?" Elsie's gaze was sharp enough to pierce his skin. Then, slowly, with the weight of incredulity laced with disgust in her tone: "Wait a minute. What you're saying is, *you* don't believe in the ghost, do you?"

He drew in a breath and chose his words. "I don't think it's wise to rush to conclusions. . . ."

"Jesus, Dad, does a freakin' *house* have to fall on you? Didn't you tell me you'd seen her yourself, talked to her, even? Did you lie about that too?"

"I didn't lie." *Don't let this fall apart,* he thought. *Don't let this delicate peace between us rupture over something as stupid as my not knowing when to keep my mouth shut. . . .*

With a huff of exasperated breath and folded arms, Elsie flopped back against the seat and fixed her eyes on the windshield. Her lips were tight.

Paul said, selecting each word with deliberation, "Elsie, look. I saw something. Experienced something. Had an apparent conversation with what appeared to be a woman from a seventy-year-old photograph. That is all I know for sure. I never said this woman was a ghost. There is absolutely no evidence to suggest—"

"Dad, what is this, a forensics lab? What are you looking for, hair and fiber?" She turned to him then, and when he glanced in her direction he saw a face that was so intent, so filled with conviction, that it broke his heart. "Dad, don't you get it *at all*? Mary Wilcox died in 1923. She stood in my bedroom and wrote her name on my window seventy years later. *You* had a conversation with her last week! So go ahead," she challenged triumphantly, "explain that!"

But it made Paul's heart beat faster even to think about it. *She's right,* he thought. *Incredible. Miracle. There* are *things beyond the ken of mortal man. Oh, Elsie, if you only knew how badly I want to believe things are that simple . . . how much I almost do believe it . . . how proud I am of you for believing it.*

And so he said, honestly, "I can't. I can't explain it."

"Don't you see what this means?" she said eagerly. "I used to think it was just, like, over, but it's not! It means people don't die; they don't die at all. They go on! It means Uncle Andrew isn't going to die at all; did you ever think of that? Don't you think Aunt Cathy needs to know about this? And Mom—all those patients she struggles to save, and how she cries when she can't . . . Don't you think *she* needs to know?"

Oh, God, Paul thought, *don't let me do this; don't let me take this away from her.* His hands were tight on the wheel as he said, "I don't think Aunt Cathy is in the mood to hear about any of this right now, hon."

He did not have to see her face to know the disappointment that filled it. "You just don't believe in anything, do you?"

A twist of the knife. "Not true. I believe in lots of things. I believe in you." He shot her a quick smile that got no response. "Elsie, listen to me. I'm not trying to shoot down your ghost theory. I'm just trying to remind you that's all it is—a theory. And as you get older you learn there are lots of explanations for everything. I may not know what the answers are right now, but I know they're out there. And I'm hoping that together, you and I can find them."

She said, looking straight ahead, "Don't patronize me. I hate it when you do that."

Another mile passed and she said with a muffled sigh,

"Great. Just when I was getting used to having someone to talk to."

His heart twisted. "Elsie, you can always talk to me."

But she didn't speak again until they had stopped for fast food, until he had finished his hamburger and she had thrown hers out, until they were on the road again in air-conditioned silence. And then she said, in a flat, dull tone, "It's never going to be like it was before, is it? With you and Mom."

And Paul felt the last pieces of the world of artificial contentment he had built around the two of them this past week crumble when he was forced to reply, because he couldn't lie to her, "No, honey. I don't think it is."

PENNY STAYED with Cathy until two A.M., but could not persuade her to leave the hospital and come home with her. She left her friend at last sleeping—or pretending to, anyway—in a cot beside Andrew's bed, and she went home alone.

She always felt strange coming into the big, empty house by herself. Her footsteps echoed on the parquet floor, and the light from the one lamp she turned on in the foyer seemed to be swallowed up by the darkness that billowed out of the rest of the house. She was hungry, but she was too tired to eat. She thought a glass of wine would help her sleep, but the ritual glass of wine when she came home from work always reminded her of Paul and that hour they always shared discussing their days. Wine seemed pointless without him to share it with.

She slipped off her shoes because she couldn't stand the echo, and she went upstairs, carrying them in her hand. The bedroom was big and comfortable and empty. Even after all these months, she had not gotten used to the feel of this house without Paul in it.

She kept thinking about what Mike had said: *If you could find a way to connect with the people you used to be, you could also find a way to connect with each other.* She thought about Cathy, sleeping on a cot beside her dying husband. She wanted to cry for them all—for Cathy, for Andrew, for Paul and Elsie and for herself—but she couldn't find the tears.

She got into bed, knowing she wouldn't sleep, and picked up the book Cathy had given her. Idly she turned the page and began to read. Less than ten pages into the text she sat up straight in bed, her fingers thrust into her hair and her eyes riveted on the page. She whispered out loud, "Oh, dear God." She reread the previous section, flipping back pages, and then scanned forward rapidly. She read intently for another few moments, and the phone was in her hand, the first five digits of the number to the lake house pressed, before she realized what time it was and she quickly broke the connection. She sat back, breathing slow and deep, and stared at the wall.

Oh, Paul, she thought. *Oh, my darling . . .*

Without even thinking about it, she had reached for him. Without knowing what she was going to say or how to say it, she had known she had to talk to him. And she had known, without a doubt or a moment's hesitation, that he would listen, and understand.

It was such a simple thing, making that connection. The hard part was deciding whether or not you wanted to. And for the first time Penny was absolutely sure of the answer.

She opened the book again and began to reread it, slowly and thoroughly, from beginning to end.

PENNY'S BMW WAS in the driveway when they arrived. She came out onto the back porch as Paul unloaded the two plastic bags of groceries, and she watched with a smile that Paul instantly recognized as tense and artificial. She was still in her work clothes—a stylish black skirt and abstract-print blouse—and she had her arms folded around a hardcover book with a faded blue cloth cover.

"Hi," he said. "We didn't expect you until dinner."

"I just got here."

Elsie marched up the steps in front of Paul, and Penny said, "Hi, sweetie. How're you doing?"

"Ask him." Elsie jerked her head backward toward Paul, and let the screen door slam behind her as she went inside.

"It's complicated," Paul answered to Penny's questioning look.

"Seems to be the day for that," she murmured, and held the door open for him.

Paul put the groceries on the counter and started to unpack them. He did not look at her. "Actually," he said, trying to sound casual, "a few things have happened around here while you were gone. We should probably talk about them."

But he spoke only to give himself something to say, because he could see the tension in her eyes, could feel it emanating off her in waves, because he knew that she had come home early for a reason, and he wanted to postpone finding out why.

She said, "Yes, of course. But, Paul—unless it's terribly urgent, can it wait? I have something I want to talk to you about."

He looked at her quickly. "Is it Andrew? Is Cathy okay?"

Penny nodded quickly. "Andrew went home this morning. Cathy is good. She has amazing strength, really." And she took a breath. "Andrew has decided to go into a hospice."

Paul's shoulders sagged, and he turned away. He put the chops and the broccoli into the refrigerator and closed the door before he said, "Well. That's it then. No chance."

"There never was, really."

In the back of his mind he heard Elsie's voice: *Uncle Andrew isn't going to die at all . . . don't you think Aunt Cathy needs to know about this?* And his heart clenched in his chest.

Don't wreck your marriage, Paul Mason.

He turned to Penny. "We need to talk," he said.

THERE WERE TIMES when a girl just had to talk to her best friend, no matter how big a jerk that friend had been, no matter how long they hadn't been speaking, no matter who was right and who was wrong in the big fight. Of course, Elsie hated to be the one to give in, but for something like this . . . she *had* to talk to Jill. She had to.

It was, after all, a *ghost*. This was big.

She closed the door on her parents' voices, and sat down on the bed with her phone to dial the long-distance number. Her heart was beating hard with excitement, and she was glad to be making up with Jill, glad she didn't have to keep this incredible secret to herself, glad to know there was someone out there who would stand by her when her parents split up and who would believe her, really believe her, about Mary.

She rehearsed what she was going to say: "Jill, it's me." And Jill would say something snotty and she would say, "Could you just stop being a smart-ass for one minute and listen to me? This is really important." And if she said anything else stupid Elsie would remind her of their pact, and *then* . . .

The phone was answered.

"Hello, Mrs. Lindsy? It's me. Elsie."

Silence. It made her uncomfortable.

She forced a little laugh and said, "I know it's been a long time, but listen, is Jill there?"

Silence for another moment, then, "What?"

Elsie cleared her throat, squirming. Mrs. Lindsy sounded odd, but then she had never been what you could exactly call friendly, and who knew what Jill had told her mother about Elsie while they were mad at each other? She said, "Could I speak to Jill, please?"

The voice that replied was cold, and slow, and hoarse, each word spoken with such deliberate venom that Elsie recoiled from the sound of them. "How . . . dare . . . you!"

Elsie stammered, "Wh-what do you mean? I—"

"How dare you call here, you crazy bitch!" the woman screamed at her. "How dare you call here and ask for my daughter!"

"I didn't do anything!" Elsie cried. "You can't talk to me like that! All I wanted to do was talk to Jill. Is she—"

"No!" the woman sobbed.

"Wh-what?"

"No, you can't talk to her; you can't talk to my Jill and you know it, you crazy bitch, because she's dead!"

Elsie stopped breathing.

"She's dead and you know it because you killed her!"

"Why are you saying this?" Elsie whispered. "Why are you . . ."

But now there was nothing but sobbing, and then some murmured voices in the background, and then a dial tone. And Elsie was still whispering, "Why are you saying this? Why are you saying this?"

She put the phone back into its cradle and backed away from it as though it had the physical power to threaten her. She backed away until her back was against the wall, her eyes fixed upon the telephone, and when she couldn't go any farther, she turned and ran.

*   *   *

THEY WENT INTO PAUL'S OFFICE and closed the door. Penny didn't want Elsie to overhear what she had to say. He thought he knew why. Now it was his own words he heard echoing in his mind: *Well, that's that, then. No chance.*

Penny turned around, still clutching the blue book to her chest. Her face looked strained. "Paul—"

"What's that?" He indicated the book.

She glanced down at the book, and put it on his desk. "It's a book Cathy sent Elsie. In a weird kind of way, it's what I wanted to talk to you about."

Then she noticed the stack of pages beside his printer and she cast him a surprised, questioning glance. "A new book?"

"Maybe." Then, relaxing his guard for just a moment, "Yes, I think so."

"It looks as though you've gotten a lot done on it. May I?" She picked up a page but waited until he nodded before she read it.

He loved having her read his work. Loved the way her neck arched and her curls fell forward, shadowing her face, and the way her eyes moved rapidly back and forth beneath lids as delicate as butterfly wings. And when she looked up he loved the honesty in her face as she said softly, "Oh, Paul. It's wonderful."

Too long. Too long since he had heard those words. And the thought that this might be the last time made his throat tight.

She carefully placed the page back atop the others, and her face softened as she looked at it. "Remember how I used to sit on the floor beside your desk and catch the pages as they came out of your typewriter?"

"Sometimes you'd catch them on the way to the trash can."

"And I'd unfold them and read them anyway. You used an

old IBM Selectric that we got at that office-warehouse closeout sale."

"Those were good times."

She said softly, "Yeah."

She drew a breath and looked up at him. "Paul, I have something to say, and it's taken me a long time—almost a year—to even know what it is I want to say, much less how to say it.

"So I would appreciate it if you would just let me get through this once, without interrupting."

Her hands were pressed tightly together, in the way she had of doing when she was nervous. He wanted to take them, and loosen them, and hold them gently in his. Instead he sat on the edge of his desk and gestured her to a chair. She declined with a shake of her head, and walked a few steps away.

"You," she said, "are the best friend I have in the world. When you betrayed our marriage, the worst thing about it was that . . . I had nobody's shoulder to cry on. No one who understood. I lost my best friend. But that's not why I hated you. I hated you because I never saw it coming. Because when we grew up we grew apart and *you* never told me. Somehow over the years I turned over the guardianship of this relationship to you, and you didn't do your job. You didn't tell me we were in trouble. That's why I hated you.

"Of course, I was blaming you so I wouldn't have to blame myself, I know that. This marriage . . . was a partnership. We each had a responsibility to protect it. You abrogated yours in an awful way. But so did I.

"So I guess what I'm saying is . . . I've been trying to figure out a way to make life make sense without you, without this thing we've created together that's our version of a marriage, a family. I can't. And I hate you for that." She looked up at him. "And love you."

He took a deep breath for the first time in over a year. Still his voice was husky as he said, "If I asked you to marry me today—would you?"

She moved her head up and down, her eyes bright with tears. "I should probably be shot for a fool, but yeah, I think I probably would."

"Maybe we can't ever completely put the past behind, but it would be good, wouldn't it, just to move forward from today?"

"We used to talk about moving here, living year-round. About me setting up private practice someplace out on the highway, for the people on the lake."

"We were young, then. Things changed."

"Maybe too much. I love this house," she said. "I think I can live here now."

Paul said, "There was something Elsie wanted me to tell you . . . about the house. Something I want to tell you." He held her gaze and did not blink. He said, "It seems we have a ghost."

"Oh, God," she said shakily, and moved into his arms. "I know."

FOURTEEN

Penny said, "I was having these nightmares . . . horrible, unspeakable dreams. Funnily enough,"—she wiped dampness from her eyes with her fingers and forced a weak grimace as she turned her head against his shoulder—"I managed to blame you for those as well. But while I was analyzing it all to death, in the way I tend to do . . . it was all in that book." She stepped back and gestured to the book on his desk.

"I don't understand. What was?"

"What happened here, all those years ago. Paul, it was awful, but I have to tell you about it." She looked at him steadily, but could not quite hide the trepidation in her eyes. "There are parts of it that will be hard for you."

"Wait." He frowned in puzzlement. "Do you mean to say that you were dreaming about something that happened here? Something you didn't know about until now?"

"That's exactly what I'm saying."

He smiled slowly, with a distant wonder in his eyes. "And I was afraid to tell you I'd seen a ghost."

She took a long breath and released it a little unsteadily. "I think . . . maybe asking someone to believe the impossible is the ultimate act of trust."

They looked at each other for a long time, unflinching and unafraid. And then Paul said, "Maybe we both have more capacity to believe the impossible than we thought we did."

"I'd like to think so," Penny said. "I just know it's not a bad thing to have your world shaken up now and then. It lets you know what you're made of."

The phone on the desk rang. She looked at it for a full three rings, but a doctor did not refuse to answer the phone, even off duty. She moved out of Paul's arms and picked it up.

"Penny, this is Newton Lindsy."

Her heart began to pound with the words. "Newton." Paul moved close when she said it, concern in his eyes. "I didn't expect to hear from you. How are you?"

"Actually I'm calling to see about Elsie. And to apologize for my wife. She was understandably upset."

"Elsie?" Penny repeated, her throat dry.

"Yes. I'm afraid she called here a little bit ago. Well, it would be bad enough, but on today of all days . . ."

"Oh, my God," Penny said under her breath. "The anniversary date." Her eyes met Paul's and she saw the same shock and anxiety reflected there.

"Look, I know the child has problems, and God knows we don't mean to add to them, but when she asked for Jill, what did you expect Rosie to say? How could you expect her to react?"

"She didn't—"

"She was quite . . . well, upset. Harsh things were said, I'm afraid. I just wanted you to know that I'm sorry, and that on any other day . . ."

"Yes," Penny said. Her hand was slippery on the receiver. "Thank you for calling. I'm sure everything will be fine." She hung up without saying good-bye.

She looked at Paul. "Where is Elsie?"

"In her room, I thought. What—"

And then he heard it, a desperate cry that he could not be certain was in his head or in the air: *Paul Mason! Come quickly!*

His eyes went to the French doors and the lake beyond. He said, "Oh, my God." And he left the room at a run.

ELSIE UNTIED THE BOAT and pushed it out of the dock. It had drifted a couple of hundred feet away from the boathouse now, on a mild current that went nowhere. In the hole left by its absence, the water was black, and when Elsie leaned over, she could see her face reflected, like a white, wavering moon in the middle of a midnight sky. They had the deepest cove on the lake, her dad said. The water there was always cold.

She was neither surprised nor pleased to see another face reflected beside hers. She sat back on her knees and looked across the narrow dock at Mary, who was not, according to her father, really there.

Mary's face looked anxious and upset. She said something, but Elsie couldn't hear.

There was a fish-cleaning table near the door of the boathouse, with a set of fillet knives in a leather scabbard. Elsie walked over and chose a knife from the scabbard, sliding it out, turning its thin, curved blade over the water.

Elsie said, "It's true, isn't it? We don't die. We just . . . go on. That should be interesting."

She looked down at the knife in her hand. "We used to talk

about ways to do it. About what it would feel like." She looked at Mary. "What does it feel like? Does it hurt very much? Or is it just like going to sleep?"

Mary reached out a hand to her, and she seemed to be speaking intently.

Elsie said, "That is so weird. Dad says he can hear you. Why can't I?"

"Because you wouldn't like what she has to say." It was her dad's voice, breathless from running, but otherwise calm. He was standing at the door to the boathouse, and followed only a moment later by her mother.

Penny drew herself up short, clutching Paul's arm, staring at the woman in a pale shirtwaist and with upswept hair who knelt across from her daughter. "Is that—"

Paul nodded, his eyes on Elsie. "She wants you to listen to her," he told his daughter.

"Oh, my God," whispered Penny. She clutched Paul's arm. "Oh, my God, Paul . . ."

"I'm listening," Elsie said. "I just can't hear." She neither tightened nor loosened her grip on the knife. But she moved her feet out from under her so that they dangled over the edge of the dock. She took off her shoes and dropped them, one by one, into the water. They were sneakers and didn't sink immediately, but floated and gasped out air bubbles like living things.

Penny sucked in a breath through her teeth and tried to keep it silent. She said, "Elsie, honey, please. What are you doing?"

Elsie looked at Mary. "What is it like, being dead?"

Penny whispered, "No," and started moving around the dock toward Elsie.

Mary looked helplessly at Paul. "Can you hear me? Please don't let her do this. Don't lose your little girl."

Paul looked quickly from Mary to Elsie. "She wants to tell you something, Elsie. She came all this way, she did this . . . this incredible thing, to tell you something."

"It's not her time to die," Mary pleaded. "Oh, please tell her that."

Penny pressed her fingers to her lips, shaking her head and staring at the apparition, through whom she would have to pass to reach her child. She found she couldn't move.

"You can see her, too, can't you, Mom?" Elsie said conversationally. "See, I'm not as crazy as you thought I was."

Elsie extended her arm and with the tip of the knife sketched a bright red line from inner elbow to wrist. Penny cried out and lunged for her, but Paul caught both her arms and pulled her back. "Don't," he said hoarsely, lips to her ear. "If she jumps, she'll be under the boathouse. I'm not sure I can get her out in time."

Elsie said to Mary, "How did you do it? Die, I mean. My friend Jill and me, we used to talk about it all the time. Stupid stuff." And she scowled, focusing on the oozing red line on her arm. "She's not my friend anymore, though."

Mary's eyes were wide and filled with pain as she reached out a hand to Elsie. "Oh, please don't do this. Don't make your mother lose her child."

Penny caught a sob in her throat, desperation tightening her voice. "What?" she said to Elsie. "What did you talk about, honey?"

But it was as though Elsie didn't hear her. Her parents had become the ghosts in her world, and her attention was focused on Mary. "How did you die?" she asked.

Mary was shaking her head, her face filled with distress. "I don't know," she said, and she looked at Paul. "Tell her I don't remember!"

Paul told Elsie quickly, "She doesn't remember, honey. It's the truth. She says she doesn't remember."

"That's odd." The droplets of blood on Elsie's arm were like tiny, perfectly formed garnets. The cut was shallow and bled slowly. She lifted the knife again.

Penny's body jerked as though it were hers that had been assaulted with the knife. She said on a hoarse, indrawn breath, "*I* know."

As one, three pairs of eyes were upon her—two living, one not. And Penny said, "I've seen it, all of it. I've dreamed what she doesn't remember."

The woman in the shirtwaist and upswept hair, the woman with anguished eyes who reached out to Penny's daughter, the woman who could not possibly be there, turned to Penny. Confusion was tangled with the anxiety on her face.

"You?" she said uncertainly. "You have my memories?"

Penny said in a tight, choked voice, "From one mother . . . to another."

Elsie was looking at her mother, and Paul squeezed Penny's arm. "Go on," he said softly, watching his daughter. "Tell her."

Penny swallowed hard, trying to focus on her words and not on her daughter, whose life now hung in the balance, just as the life of this other woman's child had done so many years ago. She made herself look at the ghost. Her voice was ridged with fear and reluctance. "It was in the kitchen, after . . . after supper. You were clearing the table. Your husband . . ."

"He was a doctor," Mary said in a soft breath, and her fingers fluttered to her lips as though to contain the awful wonder of the slowly unfolding scene. "He had been with a patient for a day and a night. . . ."

Penny swallowed hard. "It was in the book. The book Cathy had. He had just completed a cesarean section that went badly."

"Oh, yes," Mary said. Her eyes were dark now, with a remembered suffering that was terrible to behold. And as she spoke, Elsie's eyes widened, and she got slowly to her feet.

"I can hear you," Elsie said, staring at Mary. "I can hear you talking."

Paul's fingers slowly relaxed their grip on Penny's arm. He hardly drew a breath as he watched his daughter and the apparition who stood near her.

Mary spoke as though to herself, calling forth the memories strand by stubborn strand, weaving them into a reluctant whole. "She was . . . an older patient, and not . . . not a good candidate. He worried about her so. And then . . . it was such a difficult labor, almost thirty-six hours. There was nothing else to be done." Her voice rose a little then, and her eyes turned, pleading, to Penny. "If he hadn't performed the surgery, she would've died, and the baby would have died."

"But they died anyway," Penny said softly.

"There was so much blood," Mary said sadly. "Oh, it was a terrible sight, just terrible."

"So much blood," repeated Elsie, staring at her arm, and Penny's fingers dug into Paul's wrist.

Mary's hand, which had been at her cheek, dropped to her side, and she turned away. "I don't remember any more."

Elsie said, "I don't want to remember."

Penny's breath came quick and shallow. Paul hardly breathed at all.

Paul said softly, "It's okay to remember. It's the things we can't see that can hurt us. It's over now, and it's okay to remember."

It was not clear, from his words or his expression, whether he spoke to Mary or to Elsie. Perhaps it was to both.

Elsie shook her head slowly, looking at Mary. "It wasn't my fault. She said it was, but it wasn't."

Penny said swiftly, "Of course it wasn't your fault, honey; we know it wasn't. . . ."

Mary said, "It was all my fault. It was my fault that they died!" Her voice was starting to rise, and it echoed through the building like the scrape of metal on glass.

Elsie covered her ears and Paul looked sharply at Penny. "Tell her," Paul demanded. "Tell her what the book said."

Penny shook her head. "No, I can't, I—"

Mary cried, "I should have saved them; I could have stopped them, but—"

"How could I have stopped her?" Elsie shouted. "What was I supposed to *do*?"

Paul cried, "Penny, please!"

Penny drew in a ragged breath. "I know what happened," she said, loudly enough to be heard across the echo of grief that cascaded off the sides of the building. "I know how it was."

Mary turned to her with a sob, her face wrenched with sorrow. "I don't want to know! Don't make me remember!"

"Sometimes," Elsie said, "things are just too awful to remember." Tears were running down her cheeks, and she gripped the knife tightly in both hands, the blade facing her.

"I know, sweetie," Paul said. "I know. Elsie, honey, put the knife down. You're scaring us."

Elsie looked at him. "We used to talk about it all the time, did I tell you that? Well, Jill did, anyway. We had this kind of,

I don't know, club thing going on. She'd read all these really strange ways people came up with to do away with themselves and then I'd try to top them with even wilder and gorier ways to commit suicide. It was like a game, really. At least I think it was. I really don't remember."

"I know, sweetie," Paul said. Slowly he eased the pressure on Penny's arm, and he took a step toward her.

It was Mary then who flung out an arm and took a lunging step toward him. Paul staggered backward as though he had been physically pushed.

"No, stop it!" Mary cried. "Don't come here! I won't let you come here!"

Elsie cast a confused glance between her father and the ghost, and then she tightened her grip on the knife defensively.

Paul took another, quicker step toward them and again he was flung backward, this time so powerfully his shoulders hit the wall of the boathouse with a force that shook debris from the rafters.

Mary stepped in front of Elsie, shielding her with her outspread arms, and she cried, "I know you! I know your face!" Her eyes were wild, her voice hoarse with terror. "I won't let you hurt her; I won't!"

"She's my daughter!" Paul said. "I'm not going to hurt her! I—"

Penny's fingers wound tightly around Paul's, silencing him. She could feel tremors in her arm muscles, hear Paul's heavy, uneven breath. She focused on the woman who stood between her daughter and safety. She held her eyes.

"Listen to me," she said. "I know why you came here. I know what happened all those years ago. You came to remember, and I can help you."

"I don't want to remember," she whispered, anguished.

"But you must. And when you do, you will help me save my child."

"I want to save her," Mary whispered. "I only want to save her."

"Then listen to me." Penny's breath was labored, but she tried to keep her voice steady. She did not take her eyes off her daughter. "This man, the husband of the woman who died, he went crazy with grief."

"So much blood." Mary's eyes were dark with horror, her gaze upon the past.

"There was so much blood," said Elsie.

Penny felt Paul's fingers squeeze hers, quickly, urgently. She made herself go on. "He came to Mary's house, with a . . ." Her throat unexpectedly contracted and she couldn't say the word. She stared at the knife in Elsie's hand.

"I was cleaning up the dinner things," Mary said slowly. Remembrance unfolded in her eyes like churning storm clouds, and the water in the dock reflected that appearance, black and terrifying. The words came, each with a jagged edge, torn from her heart. "My baby was playing on a pallet by the stove. She was only two. She had the fattest little legs. Jeff was sitting at the table. Just sitting there, so tired. And then *he* came in, just burst through the back door, and he was screaming, 'You cut her open; you cut her open and killed her, you butcher. . . .' "

The water began to move, slapping against the dock as though in the wake of a storm, and a cold wind cut through the boathouse, stinging their eyes, rattling the poles and tackle that were hung on the walls. Mary's eyes were blank, turned deeply inward toward the past, and her chest rose and fell rapidly. Penny gripped Paul's hand and could not say a word.

Elsie spoke, clearly and conversationally and with just a

slight overtone of puzzlement, as though repeating a story she did not quite understand. The wind whipped air across her eyes and cold water splashed up to soak her feet, but she seemed unaware of the turmoil within the boathouse.

"We had this pact," she said, "this silly little pact, that we were going to, you know, try it on July twenty-third. We were supposed to go to the lake that week, remember, and she thought it would be cool to do it here, in the boathouse. But she said so many crazy things. All the drugs and stuff. Then Mom had to work and the vacation was canceled and I . . . well, I kind of forgot about it. And then I went over to her house that afternoon and there she was in the kitchen. . . ."

A small sound of strangulated pain came from the woman who was not there, and Mary whipped her gaze to Paul. "I knew you!" she screamed. "All this time I knew your face!"

Penny cried, "No, no, you're wrong!" But Mary didn't hear her; she didn't listen; she turned the full force of her horror on Paul.

"You just started slashing," Mary said. "Oh, I see it now. Blood sprayed everywhere, all over the kitchen, the cupboards and the walls and the doors. I started screaming and I fell on the floor trying to get Sarah, but she was too fast for me. She ran away, so I rolled under the table, and I tried to find her, but all I could see were footprints in the blood. . . ."

"She had cut her own throat," Elsie said. Her voice was toneless, but tears carved ragged tracks down her cheeks. "There was so much blood, so much blood everywhere, and I started screaming, 'Jill! Jill!' And I ran over to her and thought I could wake her up, thought it was a joke or something, but her skin was, like, it was *cold*, oh, my God, it was slimy and cold and she was so dead. . . ."

"My baby," Penny sobbed, reaching out a helpless arm for Elsie. "Oh, my baby . . ."

"And then I saw her little foot, peeking from behind the table legs, so still, so still." Tears, as clear as lake water, were running down Mary's cheeks. "I couldn't stop him; I couldn't save her; I couldn't save either of them. I just hid there under the table and watched the blood spatter on the walls. . . ."

Elsie looked at her mother, the knife shaking in her hand. Her voice was tiny and tight. "Mommy, I should have told you; maybe if I had told you she would be alive. . . ."

The expression on Elsie's face was a horror to behold. She looked at the churning, lashing water. She looked at the knife in her hands. She looked terrified to live, terrified to die.

Penny pleaded, "Please, move aside. Please let us go to our baby. . . ."

Mary looked at her, and then slowly at Paul. "It wasn't you . . . was it?"

Tears were like sea spray on Penny's face, soaking her collar, dripping into the corners of her mouth. She reached out her hands helplessly to Mary. "No, it wasn't. Your time is past, don't you see; it has all been done and over with for years. But this is our time, and this is our child. Please, please let me help her."

But even as she spoke Elsie threw herself forward toward the dark water. Penny screamed. Paul lunged across the dock toward his daughter and they both knew it was futile, that she would be swallowed up by the angry water and he would never find her. It all happened instantaneously, in the space between one breath and the next, in the fraction of time where two worlds intersected. As Elsie's feet left the dock but before her body touched the water, Mary caught her around the waist and pulled Elsie to safety.

Paul scooped up his daughter into his arms, and the knife fell into the lake. Penny rushed around the dock to them.

"It's okay, baby; it's okay." She said it over and over again, stroking her daughter's hair, while Elsie sobbed brokenly, hic-coughing and choking on the depth of her grief, safe in her parents' arms. Paul embraced them both, rocking them gently, his face pressed to Penny's, their hair tangled together, their breath and their tears intermingled. "It's okay," he echoed, whispering. "Everything's going to be okay."

Forever passed. The tumult eased. Elsie slowly exhausted herself with tears and Penny lifted her head, cupping her daugh-ter's face in her hands, and she said, "Listen to me, sweetheart. It wasn't your fault; nothing you could have done would have changed anything; you must believe that."

"She's really dead, isn't she?" Elsie whispered. "I don't want her to be, but she is."

"I know, baby." Paul kissed her hair. "I know."

They clung to each other for another long moment, wrapped in grief and clutching for strength. Penny plucked the damp strands of hair from Elsie's hot, wet face, smoothed the tangled mass with her fingers. She whispered, "I'm so sorry, baby. I'm so sorry you had to go through this. I'm so sorry I couldn't help you."

"It's okay, Mom," Elsie said. "You helped *her*. And I think . . . it's all the same."

For the first time Penny became aware that the wind had stopped; the water was calm. She met Paul's eyes in question and trepidation. As one they turned, and the ghost was still there, a woman in a pale shirtwaist with the scars of dried tears on her face and loosened strands of hair tumbling from her up-sweep. But the anguish had faded from her expression; the ter-ror and the wildness were gone from her eyes. She looked tired, but calm. Almost peaceful. And it was that expression, more than any other thing, that made her seem not quite as present as she had been before. She was solid and as certain as either of them. . . . And yet she was not.

Mary said, in a hushed voice, "They were killed that night, the ones I loved. And when he had finished with them, he came for me. But that wasn't what separated us. Death didn't destroy my family. I did. Because I couldn't forget the way they died, I chose instead to forget the way they lived."

Penny swallowed hard. She shifted her weight, and she spoke directly to the ghost. "You couldn't have saved your family," she said. "According to the accounts of the day, you died first. When you fell under the table, it was with a mortal wound, and there was nothing you could have done."

In the silence, the water lapped thinly against the side of the dock. Penny could hear Elsie's wet breathing, and her own, and Paul's, strong and steady. And as she watched, the surprise, even disbelief, on the face of the woman across from her slowly began to fade into wonder, and finally into gentle understanding.

"Ah," she said. Her eyes were soft now, and her head tilted slightly, as though listening to a voice they could not hear. "Ah."

Paul said slowly, "That's why it had to be us. We're her descendants, and we had to be the ones to find out the truth."

Mary looked at him tenderly. "No. My family is not here. They left this world that night. I have no descendants here."

Paul looked at Penny. She avoided his eyes for a moment. Then she looked at Elsie, and she looked at the ghost, briefly.

Penny said, "According to the book, the man who killed Dr. Wilcox and his wife and child that night . . . his name was Winston Mason. Your great-grandfather. He was apprehended by the police later that night and shot trying to run away. The police report indicated that he never realized what he had done." She found Paul's hand, and closed her own around it. "That's why she was afraid of you just now, and thought she had to protect Elsie from you. You must look like your great-grandfather in some way."

Paul stared at her, and Penny felt the horror chill him as he slowly shifted his gaze to Mary. "It was my great-grandfather? A murderer?"

"His son had been sent to stay with his uncle in Logan-town, and was only three years old when it happened. My guess is that it was never talked about in the family, and eventually just . . . forgotten," Penny said.

"I remembered your face," Mary explained simply. "Because it was the last one I saw in life. And that's why," she added, with a slow kind of wonder in her voice as though she, too, were understanding for the first time, "it had to be you."

Paul sat back heavily, looking at Elsie, at Penny, and finally at the woman who gazed down upon him with such kind dispassion. "This . . . will take some getting used to."

"It was long ago," Mary said, and a faint smile was on her face and in her voice. "In another world."

Elsie said, "It's getting harder to see you."

Paul said urgently, "Wait. There's so much we want to ask you, so many questions."

Mary's gaze seemed to be fixed on something in the distance, and her smile was gentle. "I have a life in another place. A husband, whom I sometimes called Michael, and a daughter, whom I've missed. There's nothing to keep me from them now."

Elsie said urgently, "But I need to know—"

Mary looked at her deliberately and said, "I don't have your answers. But this I know: there is no escape from this world. What you seek to leave behind, you always take with you. You go on." And then she smiled. "But when all is as it should be, you go on in a very, very different way."

She turned, then, and walked away from them, and when she reached the door of the boathouse, she simply disappeared.

Elsie turned from the empty space where Mary had been to her mother, and alarm crossed her face as she reached up a hand to wipe Penny's tears. "Mom, it's OK. Don't cry. I'm sorry I scared you, but it's all right now. Everything is going to be all right."

Penny kissed her through the tears she couldn't seem to stop, and she looked at Paul with joy and wonder in her eyes. She said, "I know, baby." She swiped a hand across her face, but the tears continued to flow, even though she was smiling now. "I know."

After a long time they got to their feet and went outside into the deepened green day, breathing deeply of the clean air. But they did not go back to the house.

Arms linked, they sank to the grass, the three of them, and they watched the sun set over the lake in silence until it, too, disappeared.

Don't miss Donna Boyd's sweeping epic of soaring suspense and dark longing

An elegant man sits in the office of Dr. Anne Kramer, confessing to a heinous murder in the highest echelons of power that has horrified the modern world.

"It began with the magic, you see. And so, perforce, must I." As a boy named Han at the House of Ra, an isolated oasis in the Egyptian desert of a far ancient time, Sontime was trained in the science of alchemy—sorcery and miracles. Only two other initiates were as skilled as he: Akan, a boy whose thirst for knowledge was matched only by his hunger for truth; and Nefar, a beautiful girl filled with wonder and ambition. Together they discovered theirs was a power unmatched in the physical world. Until the fateful moment when their alliance was forever damned, their gifts horribly corrupted. . . .

"[An] engrossing tale of magic and immortality . . . Love, jealousy, insanity, and murder all figure in this pitch-perfect narrative."
—*Publishers Weekly*